THE VAMPIRE TALON

INHERITANCE OF ASH

ROBERT AUSTIN MOWBRAY

PRINTED IN THE UNITED STATES OF AMERICA

ISBN: 979-8-9986670-4-6

ACKNOWLEDGMENTS

**Book Cover Design by Robert Austin Mowbray
In collaboration with
Book Writing Agency, US**

DEDICATION

For those brave enough to confront their shadows and seek the inner light, this book is dedicated to all dreamers and believers who pursue understanding, unity, and the courage to shape their own stories. May your journey be forever strengthened, and may the light guide your way ahead.

DISCLAIMER

TABLE OF CONTENTS

Introduction—

Prologue
Whispers in the Fog

Chapter 1
The House on Half Moon Street—1

Chapter 2
London, 1723—6

Chapter 3
Shadows Beneath the Stones—13

Chapter 4
The Gathering Fog—20

Chapter 5
Beneath the Gaslight Veil—26

Chapter 6
The Crownless Court—32

Chapter 7
The Poet and the Pale Court—37

Chapter 8
The Shadow and the Flame—42

Chapter 9
Ash and Salt—54

Chapter 10
The Silver Emissary—60

Chapter 11
The Fire That Does Not Burn—67

Chapter 12
The Storm Unleashed—73

Chapter 13
The Gathering Storm—80

Chapter 14
Valewind Pass—86

Chapter 15
Valewind Ignited—92

Chapter 16
Ash Beneath the Skin—99

Chapter 17
The Silence Between—105

Chapter 18
The Fracture that Burns—112

Chapter 19
The Black Between—119

Chapter 20
The Chains of Inheritance—127

Chapter 21
Through the Bones of the Earth—133

Chapter 22
The Space Between Hearts—139

Chapter 23
The Quiet Flame—144

Chapter 24
The Fire at Her Back—151

Chapter 25
Where the Light Fractures—159

Chapter 26
The Hollow Crown—166

Chapter 27
The Breaking Tide—173

Chapter 28
Ashes and Embers—179

Chapter 29
The Echoes We Keep—184

Chapter 30
Beneath the Silence of Ash—189

About the Author—195

Author's Other Books—196

INTRODUCTION

In The Vampire Talon: Inheritance of Ash, the fourth book in the series … London, 1720s. Fog covers the streets. Blood seeps beneath them.

Talon, the immortal warrior bound by ancient love and haunted by war, has found rare quiet in the shadowed corners of Georgian London. Beside his beloved Franco, he watches over the city's dark undercurrent, where vampire clans rule behind candlelit curtains and secret pacts.

But peace shatters when a young woman—Clarice, a wounded beauty cloaked in mystery—is brought into their sanctuary. Hidden within her veins lies a forbidden legacy: the last remnant of a blood magic long thought extinguished. As Clarice's power stirs, so too do the enemies that hunt her—the Crownless Court, a faction of exiled vampires seeking to awaken something beneath London that was never meant to rise.

Old alliances fracture. Forgotten monsters return. And as Clarice's fate entwines with Talon's, the fires of the past begin to burn again—through blood, through ash, and through love that time cannot kill.

Inheritance is not always a gift. Sometimes, it's a curse waiting to be claimed.

Prologue: Whispers in the Fog

London, 1723

The Thames rolled black beneath the moonlight, its surface slick and trembling like a serpent's back. Fog coiled through the streets, blurring gaslights and softening the edges of carriages and clipped heels on cobblestones. It was a city of masks—of powdered wigs, painted lips, and secrets stitched beneath velvet waistcoats.

Talon moved through it like a shadow.

He wore midnight black, the collar of his coat high against the wind, his boots silent despite the wet stones beneath. The curls of his chestnut hair framed a face that had not changed in over a century, save for the quiet weight that experience carved behind his eyes. In a city of performance and pretense, Talon did not need to pretend. He had outlived kings and queens, watched empires twist into new shapes, and still the hunger remained.

Franco walked beside him, his steps relaxed but alert, the very image of refined indifference. He wore a deep burgundy coat, rich against his olive-toned skin, and a smile played faintly on his lips—one that could charm a duchess or unsettle a magistrate. Together, they cut a figure the city could not quite place: too elegant for merchants, too elusive for lords. And yet, both were welcome in drawing rooms where whispers reigned and invitations bore wax seals like spells.

"They still wonder," Franco murmured, glancing toward a passing carriage whose curtains twitched with curiosity. "Who we are. What we are. It amuses them. They make stories."

"They always do," Talon replied, voice low, eyes fixed on a lamplit square ahead. "And soon, one of those stories will be too close to the truth."

They stepped onto Hanover Square just as a scream split the night. It came from the alley to the left—a raw, strangled sound choked with fear. Talon reacted first, moving swiftly down the narrow passage, the fog parting at his wake like curtains torn open. Franco was close behind, already reaching for the blade tucked beneath his coat.

What they found was no ordinary cutpurse's scene. A man lay sprawled in the muck, his throat torn open, the cobbles gleaming with arterial crimson. But there was no human thief standing over him. The creature crouched above the body had the shape of a man but none of its grace. It turned toward them with feral eyes—burning yellow, ancient, hungry.

"A Feral," Franco said, disgust curling his lip.

Talon stepped forward, voice calm but sharp. "You've broken sanctuary."

The creature hissed, backing away slightly as if it understood. Its hands were clawed, its skin marbled with dark veins. A failed turning, Talon knew. One of Ashford's legacy monsters, no doubt—beasts sired by blood without balance, created by those who fed without teaching, took without binding.

Franco moved to block the alley's mouth as Talon drew near.

"Who sired you?" Talon asked.

The creature only snarled. Then it lunged. It moved fast, but Talon was faster. His blade slid free of its sheath with a whisper, flashing silver in the moonlight. In one fluid motion, he drove it through the creature's chest. It shrieked—an awful, high-pitched wail that reverberated off brick and bone—and then went still. Its body crumbled into ash, caught on the wind.

Silence fell.

Talon stood over the remains, unmoving, until Franco's hand came to rest lightly at his back. "More of them lately," Franco said. "The blood is stirring."

Talon nodded once. "Something is coming."

They turned away from the corpse in the alley, blending once more with the fog and firelight of the street. As they walked, the sounds of the city resumed—the rattle of carriage wheels, the laughter from a brothel window, the crackle of a chimney catching flame. London lived on, blind to what stirred beneath.

But in the distance, cloaked figures watched them from a rooftop, their eyes gleaming red. And somewhere in the west of the city, beneath a crumbling estate near Kensington, something old began to wake.

Chapter 1: The House on Half Moon Street

London, 1723

The townhouse at Number Nine, Half Moon Street stood in quiet defiance of time. Its façade was clean and elegant, its iron railings freshly painted, its windows always aglow with warm lamplight—yet the city knew better than to look too closely. Servants walked quickly past it. Neighbors spoke fondly of its occupants but never invited themselves inside. Rumors bloomed like ivy around its walls. Whispers that its owners never aged. That the lights never dimmed. That music could be heard at odd hours— soft, haunting music, as if the ghosts of Paris or Florence lived there now.

Inside, Talon stood in the music room, one hand on the window latch, the other wrapped around a glass of deep crimson. His eyes were fixed on the street below, where the fog curled over gaslit cobblestones and footmen shouted for carriages. It was the Season, and London danced. At least on the surface.

Behind him, the fire cracked gently, and Franco lounged in a tufted velvet chair, thumbing through a slim volume of poetry. He wore no shoes, and his coat had been discarded across the armrest, revealing a loose white shirt open at the collar. The candlelight touched his skin like an old lover, bringing gold out of olive and shadow.

"You've been watching for nearly an hour," Franco said, not looking up. "What are you hoping to see?"

"Not what," Talon replied.

"Who." Franco sighed and set the book aside. "Still the Feral?"

"Yes. The one we killed in Hanover Square wasn't acting alone. I found a mark on the underside of its wrist—an old clan sigil. Twisted beyond recognition, but the outline was unmistakable."

Franco stood now, crossing the room to pour his own glass from the decanter on the mantel. "Ashford's legacy?"

Talon nodded. "I think more than that. Something's awakened. Something that's pulling the lost ones out of the shadows. And I believe London is only the beginning."

They drank in silence for a moment, the room still except for the soft ticking of a French clock and the wind against the windowpanes. Then Talon turned to face Franco, and his expression softened.

"You don't have to be here for this."

Franco raised a brow. "Don't insult me."

Talon crossed the room slowly, setting his glass down beside Franco's. "It's been a long time since we've known peace, Franco. Two centuries of blood. Of fleeing. Of war. You've earned rest, even if I haven't."

Franco took his hand. "And where exactly would I find that rest if not beside you?"

Their lips met briefly—warm, knowing, and without rush. It was the kind of kiss shared by lovers who had burned together and endured, whose passion still lived, but whose bond had transcended fire. Talon brushed his thumb across Franco's cheek.

"Then we stay in this together," he said.

Franco smiled. "Always."

A knock shattered the moment.

Both men turned. It was soft, deliberate—a coded rhythm. Talon moved to the door and opened it a crack. On the other side stood Madame Lysandra, her cloak soaked from the drizzle, her eyes fierce beneath her feathered hat.

"We need to speak," she said without pleasantry.

Talon stepped aside to let her in. Franco raised a brow but said nothing, offering her a cloth to dry her hands. Madame Lysandra was the leader of The Veil, a secretive alliance of immortals who had operated beneath Europe's surface for nearly a century. While not an official court, they enforced a fragile code among the older clans—silence, discretion, and balance. London was one of their recent holdings, and Talon had been invited to join after proving his loyalty through careful, quiet action.

Lysandra seated herself by the fire and fixed her gaze on Talon. "Two more bodies. Drained. Torn. Left out like warnings."

"Where?" Talon asked.

"One in Spitalfields. The other in Marylebone."

Franco frowned. "Both far apart. That feels deliberate."

"It is," Lysandra said. "They're testing the ground. Seeing what they can get away with before we respond."

Talon sat opposite her. "Do you believe it's the same creature?"

"No." She handed over a folded parchment. "Different kill signatures. Different speeds. One was elegant—almost surgical. The other was savage, animalistic. Talon… these weren't rogues. These were trained."

Talon opened the parchment. A charcoal rubbing of a sigil —twisted, corrupted, barely legible. But he knew it. "Ashford's claw," he whispered.

Franco's fingers tightened around his glass. "I thought he was dead. You saw him fall."

"I saw him burn," Talon corrected. "But ashes can stir." Lysandra stood. "I don't know what force is pulling these old evils back to the surface, but something has fractured the balance we've held. And if Ashford is somehow connected…"

"We'll find him," Talon said.

She turned to go. "Then you must start at the root. There's a place in Southwark. A former abbey—abandoned, cursed. Locals say they hear screams at night. I sent two of my best. They haven't returned."

The door closed behind her, and the silence that followed was heavier than before.

Franco moved to the window again, staring into the thickening fog. "We should have burned every trace of Ashford's line to cinders."

"We tried," Talon said quietly. "But war leaves seeds."

Outside, thunder rolled distantly over London. The sky, so often blanketed in dull gray, now churned with something darker—pregnant with storm.

Talon moved behind Franco, wrapping his arms around him and resting his chin on his shoulder. "I won't let him take anything more from us."

Franco closed his eyes. "Then we go to Southwark." Talon nodded.

Together, they would walk into the darkness once more. But this time, they would not be the hunted.

Chapter 2: London, 1723

A thick fog clung to the cobblestone streets like an old ghost that refused to lift, muffling the clatter of carriage wheels and the chatter of midnight wanderers. Lamps flickered along Fleet Street, their glow barely cutting through the gloom. The city never truly slept. London breathed in pulses—brisk and bustling by day, then slow and secretive by night. And for Talon and Franco, the night had always been their truest domain.

The house on Gough Square stood tall and narrow, its dark brick facade unremarkable by human standards, but carefully chosen. It was a place of vantage, hidden in plain sight—mere steps from Samuel Johnson's study, yet worlds apart in purpose. The lower floors passed for ordinary: a bookseller's office, the occasional patron by day. But above, the upper floors belonged wholly to the night. It was there Talon stood now, watching the fog stir below from the tall windows of the third floor.

Franco's reflection appeared in the glass beside him, golden-eyed and sharp-angled, his presence always a balm and a spark at once.

"You feel it too," Franco said quietly.

Talon nodded. "Something's shifting. The clans... they're not as settled as they pretend."

Franco moved to his side, his fingers brushing Talon's. Even after centuries, that single touch stirred something deep, ancient, and new all at once. "It's the Hollowborn. They've been seen near the Thames again."

Talon turned, eyes narrowing. "I thought the Hollowborn were driven back into the north."

"They were. But they've returned. And not just one or two. Enough to make Bishop restless. His envoy came again last night. He wants a formal meeting."

Talon's jaw tightened at the mention of Bishop—a clan leader older than most remembered, cloaked in civility and laced with menace. His reach extended across the city's underbelly, from the gambling dens of Soho to the catacombs beneath Westminster Abbey.

"They wouldn't return unless someone drew them south," Talon said. "That makes this more than just a territorial push."

Franco moved behind him, wrapping his arms around Talon's waist, pressing close. His breath was warm against Talon's ear. "Which means this isn't just about feeding grounds or honor. Someone wants war."

For a moment, the tension ebbed—just enough for Talon to close his eyes, to let himself sink into the sensation of Franco's arms around him. It was rare, the peace they allowed themselves. Rarer still in a city that watched everything from behind lace curtains and cracked shutters.

"I won't let them take this from us," Franco murmured. "Not this time."

Talon turned in his arms, drawing him into a kiss—slow, deep, claiming. They'd weathered bloodshed, betrayal, and the endless weight of time. But this was what kept them whole. Even in the shifting winds of power and the growing unrest across London's clans, this love, this fire between them, burned brighter than any torch.

When they pulled apart, it was not with reluctance, but purpose.

"Then we begin with Bishop," Talon said. "But not at his invitation. We choose the ground."

Franco arched a brow. "You're thinking of the ruins under the Charterhouse?"

Talon nodded. "They're neutral territory. Old enough to silence most blood feuds. And there's only one way in or out. We control the meeting."

———

That night, as the bells of St. Paul's echoed across the rooftops, they descended into the bowels of the city. Beneath the Charterhouse, amid ruins even the oldest Londoners had forgotten, the meeting was already unfolding. Hooded figures emerged from the gloom, shadows moving like liquid between crumbled stone and rotting wood.

Bishop stood tall among them, draped in a crimson coat that seemed to drink in the candlelight, his face ageless and expression unreadable.

"Talon. Franco." His voice was velvet over glass. "How kind of you to accept my summons."

"We didn't," Talon replied, stepping into the circle. "We summoned you."

A slow smile curved across Bishop's lips. "Ah. So bold, even after so long. What do you hope to gain by pretending the city isn't shifting beneath your feet?"

Franco's voice was steady. "We don't pretend. We prepare."

The chamber fell silent. The only sound was the faint drip of water from a stone arch above, like a ticking clock counting down to something unseen.

Talon stepped forward. "Why have the Hollowborn returned?"

Bishop chuckled, low and bitter. "Because London calls to them, as it calls to all who've tasted old power. And because someone is offering sanctuary—perhaps even blood."

"Who?" Franco pressed. "Who's risking the Accord?"

"That," Bishop said, "is what we must discover. Unless we do, the clans will fall into suspicion and violence. The Hollowborn are the first wave. But others wait."

Talon exchanged a glance with Franco. They both saw it —the flicker in Bishop's eyes, the edge in his tone. He wasn't just reporting danger. He was courting it. He wanted the fragile peace shattered. The question was why.

———

After the meeting, Talon and Franco lingered in the shadows of the Blackfriars Bridge, the river sluggish and black beneath them.

"Bishop knows more than he says," Talon muttered. "He's stirring the water."

Franco leaned on the stone ledge beside him. "If war comes, he profits. He's been waiting for an excuse."

"And now someone's handed him one."

They stood in silence, the murmur of the river blending with distant church bells. Then Franco spoke, softer now.

"You know what scares me most?"

Talon looked at him.

"Not the war. Not even the Hollowborn. It's that the more things change, the more we have to become like them to survive."

Talon stepped close, brushing a hand through Franco's dark hair. "We've lived through worse. And we're still here. Because we don't become them. We outlast them."

Franco smiled, but it was tinged with sadness. "Then we better start planning. Because I don't think the Hollowborn came alone."

———

Elsewhere, deep beneath the crypts of an abandoned church in Whitechapel, another figure watched the fog roll through the streets.

She moved like a whisper through candlelit halls, eyes glowing faintly in the dark—eyes that had seen the burning of cities and the rise of empires. Her name was Lysandra, and her blood was old, her power hidden. Behind her stood figures cloaked in ash and shadow.

"The brothers have made contact," a servant whispered. "Bishop plays his part. Talon and Franco are moving."

Lysandra turned, lips curving. "Good. Let them believe they hold the reins. Let them think they can stop what's coming."

The servant swallowed. "What if they find out—"

"They won't," she said coldly. "Until it's too late."

She turned back to the fog outside.

"The blood of kings runs through this city," she murmured. "And soon, it will run again."

Chapter 3: Shadows Beneath the Stones

London's dusk came with a wet chill, wrapping the city in a fog that rolled over rooftops and clung to cobbled streets like a shroud. Lamps flickered to life one by one, casting amber halos across slick stones and drawing out the silhouettes of passing carriages and cloaked figures. The city pulsed beneath its veneer of civility—a beast with a thousand beating hearts, some still human, many long since otherwise.

Talon stood on the narrow balcony of their townhouse on Henrietta Street, just blocks from Covent Garden, the air laden with the scent of coal smoke, wet earth, and something fainter... the metallic thrum of blood. Behind him, the drawing room glowed with firelight. Franco's voice carried softly through the open doors, deep and languid, murmuring to one of the night-borne couriers who served as their eyes in the city.

Talon was watching the square below. A man was pacing the far side, nervous, glancing behind him. Human. Frightened. Being followed.

Something stirred.

Talon disappeared into the room with preternatural grace. "He's watching again," he said.

Franco dismissed the courier with a nod, walking to him with unhurried poise. "Which one?"

"The man near the lamplight. Same scent as the one from the Opera House last week. He's either very brave... or very foolish."

Franco moved beside him, eyes scanning the night. "He's being hunted."

"Or baited."

Franco leaned in, voice a whisper just for Talon. "Shall we spring the trap, love?"

Talon turned to face him fully, their proximity stirring something more heated beneath the ever-present tension. Franco's hand found Talon's waist, sliding along his back in a possessive stroke. Their eyes met—one smoldering gold, the other a glacial blue reflecting centuries of pain and hunger. It had been over a century since their bond was sealed in blood and fury, but it burned still—deeper now, matured by war, tested by loss.

Talon's voice dropped, velvet and edged. "Not tonight. Let them think we've grown complacent."

Franco's lips curved. "Always three steps ahead."

They kissed—not in passion, but in reassurance. Their mouths met in silence, each anchoring the other against the undercurrent that had begun to swirl around them once more. Whatever hunted them now had done its research. That was no common spy below. He wore the scent of old secrets and wet parchment, like he'd spent too long in the archives of the underworld.

————

Later That Night — The Society of the Veil

Beneath the shadow of Westminster Abbey, where the stonework itself seemed to groan with memory, a forgotten crypt had been reawakened. It had once housed the dead of royal lineage, but in the early 18th century, it had become the meeting place of a far older council—the Society of the Veil.

Candles flickered across the faces of seven seated figures. None breathed. Their skin bore the pallor of the grave, though each was preserved in a different state. At the center sat Lady Isadora Greaves, High Matron of the Thamesbound Clan, dressed in crimson silk and adorned with rubies dark as dried blood.

"The Spaniards have arrived," she said without preamble. "They've taken up residence in Bloomsbury under the guise of merchant nobility."

Lord Percival Blackridge snorted, his silver brows arching over eyes as dull as old lead. "And Talon and Franco?"

"Watching. Waiting. Still dangerous."

A younger vampire at the end of the table, Elias Thorne, leaned forward. His voice held the careless arrogance of youth, though his fangs were a century old. "Then perhaps it's time we invited them in. Make them answer to our council."

Isadora's fingers tapped once against the bone-handled goblet before her. "Invite? No, Elias. We do not invite wolves to dinner. We watch their patterns. We learn their weakness."

"You won't find one," Percival muttered. "They have none left."

———

Two Nights Later — The British Museum (under construction)

Talon and Franco passed through scaffolding and unfinished halls under cover of darkness. The museum was not yet open to the public, but inside lay relics powerful enough to draw even the oldest bloodborn across oceans. Franco held up a palm as they reached the rear gallery, eyes narrowing.

"They've already been here," he said. "I smell fire-dust… and ink."

Talon moved toward the covered sarcophagus. "And something older than both."

They had come chasing whispers—an artifact smuggled out of Greece, wrapped in pagan rites, supposedly capable of disrupting vampiric senses. Talon lifted the lid of the coffin, expecting dust. Instead, he found… nothing.

Franco's voice sharpened. "It's been taken."

Before either could retreat, a flicker of movement caught Franco's eye. From behind the gallery walls emerged two figures cloaked in mourning black, faces hidden, blades drawn. Their scent was wrong—ritualistic, anointed with myrrh and sulfur.

Talon moved first, intercepting the first attacker with a spin and vicious slash of his curved dagger. Franco ducked beneath the arc of the second's blade, his movements elegant and lethal. The fight was fast, violent, almost too controlled to be random.

As one assailant fell to Talon's blade, their hood slipped back, revealing not a vampire—but a human marked with runes.

"Witchblood," Talon hissed. "A cult."

Franco knelt beside the body, frowning. "They were trained. This wasn't a theft. It was a message."

Talon crouched beside him, glancing down the darkened gallery. "Then let's answer it. Loudly."

———

Later — In the Quiet of Their Rooms

The fire crackled as they shed their weapons and coats. Blood spattered Franco's collar, and Talon caught it with a swipe of his tongue as he leaned in, tasting the night, the rage, and Franco himself.

"Did they mark you?" Franco asked, voice gravel-soft.

"No. Not tonight." Talon's lips brushed the curve of Franco's jaw. "But they've marked their intent."

Franco pulled him closer, their mouths meeting again— this time heated, urgent. Talon sank onto the settee, pulling Franco down with him, fingers threading through thick black curls as he moaned into the kiss. The world outside could burn, London could rise and fall—but here, in this moment, they were just them. Not warriors, not hunted. Lovers. Anchored.

Their passion was a dance of dominance and surrender, of tenderness and fury. The kind that spoke not only of want, but of the need to remember what was worth surviving for.

———

Final Scene — A Name Uncovered

Hours later, as the fire burned low, Talon sat wrapped in a silk robe, leafing through the pages of a stolen ledger Franco had found in the coat of one of the cultists.

"Here," he murmured, tapping a page.

Franco leaned over his shoulder, eyes scanning the name scrawled at the bottom of a coded passage:

The Order of Thorns. Founded by Lord Alaric Everwynde. Former Councilman of the Veil.

Franco's voice was sharp. "Everwynde was executed in 1665."

Talon's smile was cold. "Apparently not. Or he left behind more than a ghost."

The flames danced across his eyes as he closed the book.

"Let them come," he whispered. "Let them see what we've become."

Chapter 4: The Gathering Fog

London's midnight rain had ceased, leaving behind a glossy sheen over cobblestone streets and dripping ironwork. The gas lamps hissed faintly in the mist as though whispering secrets only the city itself could understand. The Thames churned with a soft murmur beyond the rows of buildings near Talon and Franco's residence in Spitalfields, where the scents of coal smoke and damp wool mingled with something more elusive—blood, recently spilled and not yet missed.

From the uppermost floor of their residence, Talon stood at the frost-lined window, bare-chested, the sharp angles of his collarbone catching the golden light of the fire behind him. The view revealed little—just a ribbon of fog that swallowed lamp posts and blurred the outlines of coaches below. But he wasn't looking for shape or shadow. He was listening.

"Still uneasy?" Franco's voice came soft from the bed, muffled by the folds of their quilt. The mattress creaked faintly as he sat up, pale chest exposed beneath the covers, curls mussed and eyes reflecting flickering firelight.

Talon didn't answer immediately. He watched a cloaked figure vanish around the far corner of Hanbury Street. "I can feel them," he murmured. "Someone's watching. More than one. It's like they're waiting for something."

Franco rose, slipping behind Talon and pressing his chest to his back, arms looping around his waist. "Then let them wait," he whispered, brushing his lips along the nape of Talon's neck. "They've no idea who we are."

Talon leaned into him. The bond between them had strengthened over decades, made not only by blood and shared immortality, but forged in the furnace of war, sorrow, and whispered promises beneath moonlight. Still, this city held secrets neither had yet uncovered.

He turned and kissed Franco deeply, hungrily—his hand cupping the curve of his jaw, the fire casting them in amber. When they broke apart, breathless despite their kind's absence of true breath, Talon rested his forehead against Franco's. "We've carved out a sliver of peace here," he said. "I won't let it be taken."

Franco nodded. "Then we'll defend it. Together."

———

The next night, Talon and Franco descended into the catacombs beneath St. Dunstan-in-the-East, a church that had been rebuilt more than once in its long, haunted history. The last remnants of the night's funeral rites lingered above, the scent of lilies and candle wax clinging to the worn stone. But below, deep beneath the crypts, a darker meeting was underway.

The Council of Black Thorns had summoned them.

Talon had hoped to avoid such politics, but London's vampire clans—fragmented after centuries of feuds—were beginning to stir. Some had seen what happened in the war with Ashford decades ago. Others only heard whispers. But all knew Talon by name.

A set of carved stone doors opened before them, and they entered a long, candlelit chamber where six figures sat in a half-circle. All were dressed in finery that seemed to mock time—velvets, lace, powdered wigs, and signet rings gleaming like fangs. In the center sat a woman in crimson, her black veil studded with tiny rubies like drops of blood.

"Lord Talon. Lord Franco," she greeted, her voice like silk over broken glass. "London is… honored by your presence."

Talon offered a cold nod. "You sent for us."

"Indeed." She gestured with a gloved hand toward the empty chairs before them. "Please. There are matters that must be discussed."

Franco remained standing. "Say what you mean. You're not the kind to ask politely without a dagger under your sleeve."

Several of the council members shifted, but the woman laughed lightly. "Charming as ever, Franco."

She stood then, her height commanding even among immortals. "Something is moving beneath London," she said. "Something old. Feeding in the shadows of Bethnal Green. We've lost two fledglings and a courier in the last fortnight. And their bodies... what was left of them was hollowed. As if something fed not on blood, but something deeper."

Talon narrowed his gaze. "Are you suggesting it's one of us?"

"No," she said. "Worse. Something buried. Forgotten. And waking."

———

Later that night, Talon and Franco walked the slick streets of Whitechapel, their boots tapping softly on the stones. A sense of tension lay thick in the air. Not the fear of man, which had long become background noise, but something older, like the memory of war stirring from sleep.

"Do you believe her?" Franco asked, his gloved hand brushing Talon's as they walked.

"I believe something has made even the arrogant Council of Thorns afraid," Talon replied.

They paused near a bridge, beneath which the black water of the Thames glistened like oil. The fog had thickened. Talon could hear it now, faint voices from the water's edge, murmuring in languages long dead. He looked down and saw nothing—but felt everything.

"Franco," he said, eyes locked on the rippling surface. "There's something watching from below."

A sudden scream split the air from an alley nearby. They turned as one and ran—faster than the wind, faster than thought—reaching the mouth of the alley just as the lamplight caught on a figure hunched over a prone body.

The thing was pale, not white but bleached of all color, with skin stretched thin over protruding bones. Its eyes were hollow pits, its mouth an inhuman gape filled with rows of jagged, needle-thin teeth. It hissed when it saw them and dropped the corpse like a child's toy.

Talon drew his blade. Franco moved to flank.

The creature leapt impossibly high, climbing the brick like a spider and disappearing into the fog above. By the time they reached the rooftop, it was gone.

But the body it left behind—a young woman, her eyes wide open and throat untouched—told the truth.

"She wasn't drained," Franco said grimly, kneeling. "She's still warm. But her soul… I can't feel it."

Talon exhaled, sheathing his sword. "Then the council was right. This thing doesn't just feed on blood."

Franco stood slowly. "It feeds on essence."

They stood in silence as the bells of St. Paul's tolled the hour.

Somewhere in London, the creature watched. Waiting.

And Talon realized—this wasn't the beginning of a hunt.

It was the first move in a war.

Chapter 5: Beneath the Gaslight Veil
(London, 1724)

The fog had returned with vengeance, thick and glistening with soot from the chimneys that belched over the rooftops of Spitalfields. It drifted like a living thing, curling around gas lamps and cobbled streets, swallowing the echo of footfalls. London's heart beat behind a veil—shadowy, pulsing, dangerous. And something beneath it stirred.

Talon stood at the uppermost window of their rented townhouse on Henrietta Street, his lean frame wrapped in a black brocade robe, the sash loose at his waist. His silver eyes watched the empty street below as the fog crept along the cobbles like spilled milk. He could smell the coal smoke and hear the low clatter of a carriage turning toward Brick Lane. Yet beneath that—below the surface of mortal noise—was something else. A vibration. A murmur.

Franco came up behind him, draping his arms around Talon's waist. He pressed a slow, adoring kiss into the curve of Talon's shoulder. "You haven't moved in nearly an hour," he said softly.

Talon's voice was distant. "There is something in the air tonight. It's changed. Can you feel it?"

Franco closed his eyes, breathing in the night. "Yes. It's like a low drumbeat... far away but persistent. Like we're being watched, or summoned."

Talon turned in his arms, resting his forehead against Franco's. "We need to speak with William. Whatever is coming—he may already know of it."

Franco brushed his lips to Talon's and lingered there, letting his love speak through touch more than words. "Then let's go. I won't let you face anything alone. Not now. Not ever."

———

The underground tavern known only as the Harrow's Cross stood behind a false bakery on Petticoat Lane. By day, it sold sweet buns and rye loaves to unsuspecting locals. By night, it was a gathering ground for creatures who did not fear the dark but were born of it. The door to the basement creaked open as Talon and Franco descended the narrow steps. Inside, the tavern buzzed with low murmurs and flickering candlelight. Familiar faces turned toward them—ancient, pale, and watchful.

William Godfrey, their old ally and mentor, sat at a long table at the far end, a heavy book open before him, maps and parchment strewn about. His silver-blond hair was tied back, and his dark waistcoat shimmered faintly with embroidered sigils. A goblet of bloodwine rested at his elbow, untouched.

"Talon," William said, standing as they approached. "Franco. I feared you might not come until it was too late."

Talon's voice was quiet but firm. "We feel it too. The city is uneasy. Something moves beneath it."

William gestured to the map. "It began in Southwark. Five bodies drained within a single week, all with signs of ancient feeding. But none of our kind claimed them. No signature, no allegiance. And last night..." He turned the map slightly. "There was another."

Franco leaned in. "Where?"

"Greenwich," William replied. "By the observatory. And it wasn't just feeding—it was a message."

He unrolled a smaller page. It depicted a symbol drawn in blood: a jagged crown pierced by two fangs.

Talon stiffened. "That's not just a mark. It's a declaration."

William nodded grimly. "An old faction. English-born. Thought dead after the Puritan purge in the last century. They called themselves The Crownless Court. Exiled by the original clans loyal to the Old World. They hate us, Talon. All of us. They've waited in the catacombs and the marshes. And now, they rise."

Franco glanced to Talon. "What do they want?"

William's voice was grave. "To reclaim the blood-right they believe was stolen from them. To take London. And to tear down every clan who stands in their way."

———

Later that night, Talon and Franco stood alone beneath the arches of the Southwark Cathedral crypts. The flicker of their lantern cast distorted shadows on the old stones, and the air smelled of damp moss and ancient dust. A breeze moved where no breeze should, whispering past them like a ghost in confession.

Franco knelt beside a slab cracked by time. Scratched into its surface was the same symbol: the crown and the fangs.

"They're leaving warnings," Franco said quietly.

"No," Talon answered. "They're leaving promises."

A presence stirred behind them. Talon whirled, fangs bared—then stopped.

The figure who stood there was neither ghost nor foe. Dressed in fine 18th-century attire, his powdered wig slightly askew, was a man Talon had once met in another century, in another war. A man who should have been long dead.

"Forgive the intrusion," the man said, voice smooth with cultured cadence. "My name is Alexander Pope. I imagine you've read my work."

Franco blinked. "The poet?"

"The very one," Pope said with a dry smile. "And no ordinary man, as you've likely gathered. My works were merely a distraction. The truth lies below the verses."

Talon narrowed his eyes. "You're one of them?"

Pope gave a bow, but it lacked mockery. "I was once an observer. Now, I am a messenger. The Crownless Court has sent word. They will rise with the full moon over the Thames. You must be ready. They are not interested in negotiation. Only reclamation."

"And whose side are you on?" Franco asked.

Pope's smile faded. "I am on the side of order, and survival. And I believe your union, Talon and Franco, may be the last thread holding that order intact."

With that, the poet turned and vanished into the crypt's darkness.

———

Back in the sanctuary of their home, Talon and Franco sat in silence. The fire crackled low. Franco traced a finger along the scars on Talon's chest, relics from centuries of war and survival.

"I don't want to lose you," Franco whispered. "Not in some blood feud born of ashes."

Talon pulled him close, pressing a hand to Franco's heart. "Then we stay alive. We fight together. We protect what we've built."

Their kiss that followed was not soft. It was desperate, alive, full of memory and defiance. They clung to each other in the flickering dark, as thunder rumbled across the rooftops of London.

The storm had begun. And the Crownless were coming.

Chapter 6: The Crownless Court

A restless fog had settled across the rooftops of Soho, smothering the streets in a muted hush as if London itself held its breath. It was not the usual damp veil of English mist, but something older—older and wrong. It curled unnaturally low through alleyways, slipping between the bones of the city like an unspoken warning.

Talon stood in the doorway of a bookbinder's shop just off Wardour Street, the yellow lamplight from inside catching the edge of his pale cheekbone. He watched the passersby, most oblivious, but a few glanced into the fog with furrowed brows, their instinct pricked by something they couldn't name. Franco moved beside him, his fingers gently grazing Talon's wrist in a private reassurance. They had grown skilled at the smallest touches that carried volumes.

"They've crossed the river," Franco murmured, his breath warm against Talon's ear. "Twice now, I've felt it. Not Ashford's remnants—these are new. Purposeful. Cold."

Talon's gaze narrowed. "The same ones who left bloodless corpses in Bethnal Green?"

Franco nodded. "And now there's talk in Mayfair. Poets with hollowed eyes. A baron's daughter who walked into the Thames and never came back up."

They had ruled out rogue fledglings. These were no accidental turnings. No signs of inexperience. Each victim bore the signature of precision. It was as though someone were recruiting—but not to any known London clan. Not to the old Courts of Albion. Not to the hidden enclaves of the North.

"Let's go," Talon said, his voice low and resolute. "The docks first. Then St. Giles. I want to smell the air myself."

But the night had other plans.

As they turned the corner onto a narrow lane crowded with fishmongers' crates and dirty canvas tarps, Franco suddenly stopped. His hand went to Talon's chest, halting him like a sentinel sensing a ripple in time.

"What is it?" Talon asked.

Franco didn't speak. Instead, he raised his hand and pointed upward. There, on a slanted roof three floors above, stood a man in a long dark coat, unmoving. His outline blurred with the fog but his presence rang loud in Talon's instincts—an ancient coldness wrapped in tailored civility.

Talon's eyes met the figure's—and the man smiled.

Then he simply vanished.

No blur. No leap. Just gone, like smoke pulled through a crack in the world.

"Did you see his eyes?" Franco asked, voice still hushed.

Talon nodded. "Silver. Like coins left too long in frost."

———

The figure on the rooftop was no hallucination.

Two nights later, the vampire known as Alaric appeared at an old Masonic lodge in Clerkenwell. He wore no insignia, carried no visible weapons. But he walked straight into the heart of a known neutral meeting ground for vampire clans with the air of a man taking his place at the head of a table.

Talon and Franco entered cautiously, cloaked in the formality required of such spaces. The lodge hall, long disused by mortal hands, still bore the strange geometry of its previous owners—ceilings that slanted toward hidden peaks, doorways that felt ever-so-slightly too tall, as if built for something more than human.

Alaric stood near the hearth, nursing a goblet of deep crimson. He turned as they approached, and his expression, while cordial, held the faint trace of amusement.

"You're not as tall as I was told," he said to Talon. "But you look the part."

"And you are not as polite as one would expect," Talon replied coolly.

"Politeness is currency for those who still beg favors," Alaric said, sipping. "I have no debts in this city. Not yet."

Franco stepped forward. "You're not of the old lines. Not Albion. Not the Coven of St. James. So what are you?"

Alaric set down his goblet.

"I am the echo of something this city forgot. We are the Crownless Court. And we are here to remind London of what it means to fear its own streets."

His smile spread—not mocking, but calm. Too calm.

"We do not seek permission," Alaric continued. "Only observation. Tell your allies. Tell the hidden ones. And tell the tired, self-appointed kings of faded courts to sleep lightly. Because we're not interested in councils or treaties. We are interested in blood and legacy. And this century is ours."

———

Later that evening, in their private residence overlooking the edge of Hyde Park, Franco sat before the fire, staring into the red-lit embers as Talon paced behind him.

"He's not lying," Franco said finally.

"No," Talon agreed. "But that doesn't mean he's telling the full truth."

"They're organized. Not some reborn Ashford cult, not wild fledglings. There's a structure behind him."

Talon moved to Franco's chair and placed his hands on Franco's shoulders, grounding both of them in silence for a long moment.

"They know who we are," Talon murmured.

"Yes."

"And they're not afraid."

Franco tilted his head back so he could look up at his beloved, the firelight casting gold into the shadows of his dark eyes.

"Then they should be," Franco whispered.

Talon leaned down, his mouth finding Franco's in a kiss that began tender and grew desperate. The fear, the fury, the ancient ache of loss stirred between them. But they clung to one another as if it was their only anchor, as it always had been.

No matter what empires rose, what enemies whispered in the fog—this was theirs.

The storm could come. But they would not face it alone.

Chapter 7: The Poet and the Pale Court

Rain had begun to fall just before midnight, fine as silk and cold as memory. It misted the cobblestones of Twickenham into mirrors, reflecting oil lamps and fractured moonlight, blurring the line between earth and sky. The Thames, swollen and black, whispered along the banks as if conspiring with unseen things.

Talon and Franco moved with practiced quiet along a path of crushed gravel and dormant lavender, their boots making no more noise than a breath. Before them rose a house—modest in size, with ivy climbing its flanks and candlelight flickering behind diamond-paned windows. It was a poet's home, but tonight, it hosted more than verse.

"I still think this is reckless," Franco murmured, eyeing the shadows near the hedgerows. "Pope keeps company with dangerous men—dukes, philosophers... and now vampires."

"Exactly why we must hear him," Talon replied, his voice as calm as the rain. "He's woven himself into the mind of London's elite. If he's being courted by the Crownless Court, we need to know."

Franco said nothing more as Talon rapped lightly at the door with the back of a gloved hand. Moments later, a stooped manservant opened it, blinking as though expecting no one.

"Mister Pope is not receiving guests," the man said flatly.

Talon tilted his head slightly. "Tell him Talon of the Valewind Line has come. And that the storm we feared has finally arrived."

The servant blinked again, slower this time. Then he stepped aside wordlessly.

The study smelled of leather-bound books, pipe smoke, and the musty drift of ink. Alexander Pope, diminutive and curved with the scoliosis that dogged his life, stood before a small writing desk littered with half-finished lines and spilled ash.

He turned slowly. "So the legends breathe," he said in a voice as fine and sharp as a blade's edge.

"I breathe more often than I like," Talon replied, stepping forward. "I've read your Essay on Criticism. Clever. Cruel."

"I've written worse," Pope muttered. "And you've come to warn me."

Franco closed the door behind them. "We've come to ask what you know."

Pope chuckled. "So the vampire walks through my door and expects the poet to spill secrets. You may drink from veins, Talon, but I drink from minds. And the Crownless Court pours a heady vintage."

Talon's smile didn't reach his eyes. "What have they offered you?"

Pope didn't answer at first. Instead, he walked to the hearth and tossed in a page. The fire licked it up greedily, casting a flickering glow that deepened the hollows of his gaunt face.

"Immortality," he said finally. "In words. In breath. They offer something no man has ever refused."

"But you haven't accepted," Franco noted, stepping closer.

"No," Pope said. "I am vain, not stupid."

He turned, face grim. "They've moved beneath the Houses of Parliament. Rented a chapel in Shoreditch for public gatherings. And there's something else—they're collecting relics. Ancient things. Bones. Scrolls. A crown that once belonged to someone not born of man. They believe they are the last true aristocracy of blood."

Talon's jaw tightened. "What are they planning?"

Pope's voice dropped. "To claim London. Not merely the shadows. The city itself. Its memory. Its myth."

There was a silence as heavy as lead, broken only by the rain.

"I've said more than I should," Pope whispered. "If I disappear—"

"You won't," Talon said softly. "You have our protection."

The poet snorted. "You are two."

"We've survived worse," Franco replied. "And so will you, if you keep writing truth."

———

Outside, as they crossed a garden wet with rain, Franco took Talon's hand in his. The moment was quiet—no words, only the warmth of palm to palm, the squeeze that said: I am here.

But their solitude was shattered by a cry—sharp, distant, and unmistakably inhuman.

Talon was already moving, cloak sweeping like wings behind him. They cleared the hedges in seconds, descending toward the river path where the moan had come. At first, they saw only mist and water. But then, by the embankment wall, they saw her.

A girl. No more than fifteen. Pale as chalk, eyes rolled white in her skull. Her body convulsed in the arms of a man dressed in a black coat—fine, tailored, and blood-spattered.

Alaric.

He looked up as they approached, his lips red with her blood. A half-smile curved across his face.

"She begged for poetry," he said, lowering the girl gently to the stones. "So I gave her verse."

Talon lunged, steel flashing from beneath his coat. But Alaric vanished in the fog, leaving only the girl's body and a whisper of laughter behind.

Franco fell to his knees beside her. The girl was not dead —yet. Her pulse fluttered like a trapped moth.

"She's changing," Franco breathed. "No clean kill. He made her suffer."

Talon knelt beside him. "We can save her."

But even as he said it, the girl's body arched, mouth opening in a soundless scream. Her eyes flared red, then faded to black.

"She's not his first," Franco whispered.

"No," Talon said, standing. "And she won't be his last."

They looked out over the river, where the fog grew thicker, reaching across the water like fingers seeking the throat of London.

Chapter 8: The Shadow and the Flame

The fog lay thick across the South Bank, clinging to the cobblestones like a breath held too long. It was past midnight, and London had quieted, save for the occasional drunken stumble from a nearby tavern and the restless creak of mooring ropes along the Thames. Franco moved through the mist as easily as a ghost, his long coat trailing behind him, his senses alert. He had fed earlier, and his thirst was tempered, but something in the night called to him—a whisper he could not ignore.

He heard it before he saw her. A wet gasp, sharp and desperate, as though someone had been submerged too long beneath stormy waters. He turned a corner into a narrow alley and there she was—collapsed beside a crate, her body twisted in pain, her dress torn and soaked with blood. Her chest rose in shallow bursts, and her hand weakly clutched at her side where blood pooled beneath her. The scent of it was heavy, sweet and rich, but laced with something deeper—terror, yes, but not just human. There was a trace of resistance in her, of something unbroken.

Franco crouched beside her. Her skin was as pale as snow, yet flushed from her fevered state. Her long dark hair was matted and tangled, a halo of shadow around her face. But it was her eyes that struck him when they fluttered open— gray-blue like the breaking dawn, fierce even through the haze of her pain.

"Don't..." she rasped, a weak attempt to push him away. "Please."

"I'm not here to hurt you," Franco said gently. He touched her forehead and found it burning. "You've lost too much blood. Who did this to you?"

Her eyes flickered toward the shadows behind him. "They're still out there."

Franco glanced over his shoulder, but the alley remained still. Whoever had done this was long gone—or clever enough to retreat when he approached. He slid one arm beneath her knees, the other around her shoulders. She gasped again as he lifted her, but did not resist.

"I'll take you somewhere safe," he murmured. "Try not to sleep."

She said nothing, her head collapsing against his shoulder as he carried her into the night.

———

Talon stood by the hearth when Franco returned, firelight dancing across his face. He turned slowly as the door opened and his expression darkened at once.

"You've brought someone here," he said flatly.

Franco closed the door behind him, brushing past the warm air and into Talon's tense presence. "She was bleeding out in the streets, Talon. She would have died if I left her."

"That may have been her fate," Talon said, stepping forward. "We are not saviors."

Franco laid the girl—no, the woman—upon the chaise near the fire. Her breathing had grown more erratic, and her blood had soaked into his shirt. He removed his coat and covered her with it, glancing back at Talon. "She was attacked. Someone wanted her dead and didn't finish the job."

Talon's gaze swept over her. His nose twitched at the scent. "She's not just human."

"I know," Franco said. "That's why I brought her here."

Talon paced slowly around the room, his eyes never leaving the girl. "You risked exposing us for a stranger."

"She's more than a stranger. I felt something... a pull. She's strong, Talon, and there's something in her blood. I don't understand it yet, but I couldn't leave her."

"You've always had a tender heart," Talon murmured, now standing at the head of the chaise. He leaned over, inhaling deeply near her neck, not biting—just listening with his senses. "There's magic in her," he said at last. "Old, but dormant. Someone tried to destroy her because of it."

"She said they were still out there."

Talon's jaw tightened. "Then they'll come again."

Franco approached, laying a hand on Talon's arm. "We'll be ready."

For a moment, they stood in silence, gazes locked. Talon searched Franco's face, something unreadable flickering in his eyes. "You care for her already."

Franco hesitated. "No... not like that. But I couldn't let her die."

"She's beautiful," Talon said, his voice quieter now. "And dangerous. Be careful, Franco."

Franco stepped closer still, his hand now resting against Talon's chest. "She won't come between us."

Talon's eyes darkened, but not with anger. With something deeper—longing, fear, and a storm of emotion he rarely let surface. He leaned in and kissed Franco, his mouth firm, searching. It wasn't gentle—it was a warning and a promise, all at once.

"She better not," Talon whispered, pulling back just enough to brush his forehead against Franco's.

———

The woman slept through the day, though her fever lessened and the wound began to close with unnatural speed. By evening, she stirred.

Franco sat beside her when she opened her eyes again. She startled, reaching for something—a weapon?—but her hand only clutched air. "Easy," he said. "You're safe."

Her gaze darted around the unfamiliar room, then settled on him. "Where am I?"

"In my home. London."

She touched her side and winced. "I... remember the alley. You carried me?"

"Yes."

She blinked, then studied him with growing clarity. "You're not human."

"No."

She nodded slowly. "Neither am I... fully."

Franco smiled faintly. "I guessed."

"My name is Clarice," she said. "I was born in Avignon… but I haven't called it home in many years."

"Who hurt you?"

Her lips pressed into a thin line. "They're called the Whisperers. A sect of blood sorcerers. I escaped them once. They found me again."

Talon entered then, silent as a shadow, and Clarice froze. Her eyes narrowed at him. "You're his mate."

"I am," Talon said without flinching. "And you're trouble."

Clarice arched a brow. "That's generous."

Franco stood, placing himself slightly between them. "Clarice, this is Talon. We both live here."

Clarice studied Talon for a long moment. "You don't like me."

"I don't trust you."

"Wise," she said.

And then, to Franco's surprise, she smiled.

Clarice remained asleep for two days. Franco never left her side, not even when Talon beckoned him to rest or feed. He watched over her as one would a sacred flame, worried that if he turned his gaze for even a moment, she might vanish like mist in the morning sun. Talon's concern was genuine, but he masked it beneath an air of icy restraint. His possessiveness over Franco warred with the stranger's sudden presence in their haven. He watched from a distance, studying Clarice with the eyes of a predator who had not yet decided whether to protect or destroy.

When Clarice finally stirred, it was with a hoarse gasp, her limbs flailing beneath the silken sheets of the guest chamber. Franco was immediately at her side, soothing her with a gentle hand on her shoulder.

"You're safe," he whispered. "You're in my home, in London."

Her eyes were wide, feral at first. A soft grey-green, like moss after rainfall, clouded with pain and confusion. She blinked several times, then focused on Franco's face, her voice gravelly and cracked. "Where... am I? Who—?"

"I found you," he said gently, "in the alley behind the old cemetery. You were... torn apart. What happened to you, Clarice?"

She blinked again at the sound of her name. "Clarice," she echoed softly, tasting it like a forgotten word. "I remember..."

Talon stepped into the doorway, arms crossed, face unreadable. "She remembers now," he said coolly. "How convenient."

Franco shot him a glance. "Talon—"

But Clarice raised her hand. "No, he's right to question me. You both should. I... I didn't expect to survive."

Franco leaned closer. "Who did this to you?"

She took a long breath, one that seemed to pull from something far deeper than lungs. "I escaped them. The Whisperers."

That name fell into the room like an arctic wind.

Talon stepped forward, suddenly less detached. "The Whisperers? They're little more than ghost stories— shadows in darkened corners."

"No," she said, sitting up now, trembling. "They're real. And they're here. In London."

She stared into the hearth, the flames flickering across her bruised face, illuminating the places where her skin had not fully healed. "I was raised in the Fens of Cambridgeshire. My family... my mother was the last known bearer of blood-chanting. An old magic. Forbidden, almost extinct."

Franco frowned. "You're a blood witch?"

Clarice shook her head. "I was never trained. My mother hid it well—until they came. The Whisperers found her. She was one of the last living vessels of that blood magic, and they wanted her secrets. When she refused, they made an example of her. I was only a child. I saw everything. They took her tongue. Her hands. Her life."

The silence in the room was thick. Even Talon didn't speak.

"I was hidden away by a sympathetic midwife—an old vampire loyal to the Crown who still believed in protecting our kind. She raised me in secret, taught me to keep quiet, to bury what I was. But when she died... I wandered. I thought the Whisperers had forgotten me. I thought... wrong."

Franco knelt beside her now. "They came for you?"

Clarice nodded. "Just after dusk, two nights past. They were different than I remembered. Quieter. Deadlier. I heard them whispering to each other before they struck. They knew my name. They knew what I carried."

"What you carry?" Talon asked, voice low.

Clarice turned to him, weary but fierce. "My mother's blood magic didn't die with her. It slumbers within me. I can feel it... pulsing, especially since the attack. Like something inside me woke up. I don't know how to control it. I never asked for it."

Talon's face had changed, his stoicism now edged with something like wariness—or perhaps awe.

Franco sat beside her on the bed. "You're safe here. We'll protect you."

Clarice's eyes locked with his. "I saw you in a dream. Before you found me. There was fire all around, and you reached out your hand. I didn't know who you were then, but I do now."

Franco stilled. "A dream?"

She nodded. "It wasn't just a dream. It was a pull. Something ancient. I think... your blood called to mine."

Talon exhaled sharply. "That's impossible."

"Is it?" Clarice asked softly. "You and Franco aren't bound by coincidence. I can feel it—whatever you are, whatever you share, it's part of something larger. Something... coming."

The fire crackled in the hearth, casting uneasy shadows.

Clarice stood, her legs shaking, and Franco moved to steady her, but she waved him off. "No. I need to stand."

"You need rest," Franco said.

"I need answers," she replied.

Talon stepped forward. "And you think you'll find them here?"

Clarice met his eyes evenly. "I think you and Franco are not what you seem. And I think you're exactly what I've been waiting for."

She turned her eyes to Franco once more. "You said I was safe here. I need you to mean that."

Franco's voice was soft but unwavering. "You are."

Talon turned away, tension etched into his shoulders as he left the room.

Later, after Clarice had fallen back into a restless sleep, Franco found Talon standing in the library, a glass of crimson liquid in his hand, staring into the long mirror mounted above the fireplace. Their reflections shimmered like memories—half-there, half-lost.

"You don't trust her," Franco said.

"No," Talon replied. "But I trust you."

Franco moved behind him, wrapping his arms around Talon's waist. "She's a girl who lost everything. If she's tied to something greater, then so are we."

Talon leaned back into him. "I just wanted peace. A quiet century. Is that so much to ask?"

Franco chuckled against his neck. "You've lived for centuries. Since when have your nights ever been quiet?"

They stood like that for a while, bodies close, breath mingling—two immortals momentarily at ease. But even in that stillness, they felt it: the stirring of something vast beneath the surface. Clarice's arrival was no accident. She was a thread in a web long in the spinning, and soon, the past they had buried deep would claw its way back into the moonlight.

Chapter 9: Ash and Salt

Clarice woke before the sun had set, sweat dampening her brow though the room was cold. Shadows stretched across the walls of the guest chamber, the fire long since burned down to red embers, and the window shutters creaked softly with the wind. She sat up slowly, her ribs still sore, and for a long moment, she simply breathed. Something inside her had shifted. Not in the wound—no, that had closed almost completely—but in the marrow, in her blood.

It thrummed.

She could feel it with every beat of her heart, a pulsing current of something old and primal. Not power exactly—at least, not yet—but the weight of inheritance. Her mother's voice rang in her ears, not spoken, but remembered: Your blood is a lock, Clarice. One day, someone will come for the key.

She pushed the quilt aside and rose to her feet. Her legs were stronger than they had any right to be after what she had endured, and her senses felt sharper—sight, smell, even the faintest quiver in the air. She moved to the looking glass and studied her reflection. A long scratch still marred her cheekbone, but beneath it, her eyes burned with new clarity.

There was no going back.

The door creaked open behind her. She turned to find Franco standing in the hall, arms crossed lightly, watching her.

"You're up," he said.

She gave him a tired smile. "I don't sleep easily anymore."

"Neither do we."

He stepped into the room and handed her a glass. She sniffed it—tea, spiced and slightly bitter. She drank it gratefully.

"I feel different," she said softly.

"You are," Franco replied. "Whatever the Whisperers tried to destroy… they only woke it up."

Clarice nodded. "I know."

Downstairs, Talon paced. He hadn't slept either. His mind was clouded with visions he could not place: a forest burning in the distance, voices in a language he had not heard since the fall of Constantinople, a silver dagger turning slowly in midair. Every time he closed his eyes, he saw Clarice's face—torn, bloodied, and shining with something that terrified him.

He didn't hate her. That much he'd admitted silently to himself. But she was dangerous. Not just because of what lived inside her, but because of what she stirred in Franco. Hope. Sympathy. A softness Talon feared would be their undoing.

The knock at the door came just after sunset. Sharp. Precise.

Talon was already moving as Franco descended the stairs. Clarice lingered behind, half-hidden in the shadows of the hall.

When Talon opened the door, a chill swept into the foyer.

The figure who stood there wore a cloak of indigo velvet, the hood drawn low. But even beneath the shadowed cowl, the eyes shone—amber, ancient, rimmed with violet. The scent that came off him was neither mortal nor vampire. It was earth. Fire. Salt.

Talon's hand was at his side, ready for the blade.

The visitor spoke first.

"My name is Elowen," he said, lifting his hood. "I bring a warning. And a gift."

Franco appeared at Talon's side, frowning. "A warning?"

"Yes," Elowen said. "About her."

Clarice stepped forward. "Me?"

He turned to her, and for a moment, something unspoken passed between them. Recognition? Memory?

"You carry more than magic, Clarice," he said. "You carry lineage. The blood in your veins isn't just a remnant of witches. It's the last root of a tree the Crownless Court has been trying to cut down for centuries."

Talon's eyes narrowed. "And who are you to know this?"

"I was once their ally," Elowen said. "Centuries ago. Before they turned on their own. Before they drank the sea."

Clarice's brow furrowed. "Drank the sea?"

"They drowned their bloodline," he said softly. "Bound it to the salt and ash of the old world. You are what's left."

He turned to Talon and Franco.

"She is the key to something they buried beneath the city. Something that must remain forgotten. If they take her, they will not just rise. They will rule."

Clarice stepped closer to him. "What do they want from me?"

Elowen's eyes shone brighter now. "To open what was sealed in fire. To unleash what should never rise again."

Talon's hand fell from the hilt of his blade. "Then we keep her from them."

Elowen nodded. "They've already sent their first emissary. He wears no name. Only silver rings. If you see him, run."

Franco raised his chin. "We don't run."

"You might, when you see what follows him."

Elowen pulled something from beneath his cloak and placed it on the entryway table. A small vial, sealed in wax and wrapped with a strand of silver wire.

"This is what your mother died to protect, Clarice. Her blood. Distilled and bound to old rites. If you drink it... you will awaken fully. But it will cost you."

Clarice stared at the vial. "What?"

"Whatever innocence you still have."

Talon's voice was sharp. "We're not ready."

Clarice met his eyes. "We might not have time."

And as Elowen turned and disappeared into the night, leaving the scent of storm and salt in his wake, the household fell into silence. The fire cracked in the hearth, and the shadows of the past leaned in closer.

Clarice held the vial in her hand, and her blood—her mother's blood—sang like thunder in her veins.

Chapter 10: The Silver Emissary

Rain swept across the rooftops of London like a slow mourning veil, soaking chimneys and stone gargoyles in silence. The city's pulse, steady and smog-choked, was beginning to quicken. It throbbed beneath the cobblestones and in the shadows of closed doors. Those attuned to it—the nightwalkers, the forgotten, the damned—could feel it in their bones.

Clarice stood before the hearth in the guest chamber, the vial of her mother's blood cradled in her hand. The fire flickered, casting a soft red glow through the glass, igniting the crimson liquid with an otherworldly shimmer. It seemed to pulse with a will of its own, and every beat of her heart echoed back in its rhythm. She had not slept. Could not. Her mother's voice had returned to her in flashes—whispers over wind, a name spoken through blood: Elowen... awaken the line... before they do.

Talon entered without knocking.

His presence was cool, measured. He said nothing at first, only watched her with arms crossed, his coat still damp from his patrol. He smelled of rain and iron and old war.

"You haven't touched it," he said.

Clarice turned toward him. "No."

"Why?"

She looked back at the flame. "Because once I do, I won't be myself anymore."

Talon approached slowly, boots tapping against the wooden floor. "You're not yourself now. They made sure of that."

She glanced up at him, his silhouette painted against the golden glow. "Would you take it? If it were your blood?"

"I've taken worse," he said, and for a moment, his eyes held a glint of grief so ancient it silenced the room.

Clarice's voice softened. "Franco believes I can survive this."

Talon's lips curved, but the smile didn't reach his eyes. "Franco believes in everyone. That's what makes him dangerous."

She stared at him. "And what do you believe?"

He stepped closer now, until they were nearly eye to eye. "I believe the world ends in silence and ash. I've seen too much to believe in prophecy."

Clarice held the vial tighter. "Then why help me?"

He didn't answer.

Behind them, footsteps descended the stairs—measured, elegant, familiar.

Franco appeared in the doorway, his hair damp, his eyes already moving between them. "It's begun," he said.

Talon turned. "Where?"

"Temple Bar," Franco replied. "One of the Veil's agents was found hanging upside down from the arch, drained— but not of blood. His soul was burned out. His eyes were... silver."

Talon's mouth tightened. "He's here."

"Who?" Clarice asked.

Franco answered. "The emissary of the Crownless Court. Elowen said he wore silver rings."

Clarice stepped forward. "Then we go after him."

"No," Talon snapped, sharper than intended. "We don't pursue him. He's not bait. He's a message. If we follow, he'll lead us to ruin."

Franco placed a hand on Talon's shoulder. "Then we don't follow him. We draw him in."

———

The plan began that night, beneath the city's oldest chapel: St. Bride's, a narrow stone cathedral that sat atop layers of forgotten tunnels. By torchlight, Franco and Talon opened a sealed passage beneath the crypt—a space that once served as a hideaway for persecuted monks, now repurposed as a command chamber.

Maps lay unrolled across a massive table. Inked symbols marked known safe houses, clans loyal to the old courts, and new ones whose allegiances were unclear.

Clarice stood at the far side, the vial tucked into a pocket sewn inside her cloak. She had not taken it—yet—but its presence felt heavier by the hour.

"We've confirmed the Crownless have taken two blood sanctuaries," Franco said, drawing a line between Southwark and Shoreditch. "They're moving outward like a rot."

Talon traced a path between the old Roman walls. "They're avoiding the river. Whatever they're building, it's inland. They fear the water."

Clarice spoke. "That's why they drowned their own line. To bind the power beneath it. Water holds blood."

Franco looked at her. "And your blood may be the key."

She nodded slowly. "If I drink this, they'll feel me. I'll shine like a beacon. But it will also give me power they can't predict."

Talon met her gaze. "It will change you."

"I know," she whispered. "But if I'm to survive this, I have to stop pretending I'm the same girl who ran from them."

———

Three nights later, they made their stand at the ruins of Winchester Palace, a crumbled relic of old London that now stood open to sky and storm. Clarice stood at its center, cloaked in shadow, her heart pounding. In her hand, the vial gleamed under the full moon.

"I'm ready," she said.

Talon watched her from the edge of the ruin, his sword unsheathed. Franco stood beside her, offering his hand. She took it.

Then, slowly, deliberately, she uncorked the vial.

The blood touched her lips and fire erupted behind her eyes.

She collapsed to her knees, clutching her chest, her scream echoing through the ruins like a bell tolling for the dead. Talon moved toward her, but Franco held him back. "Let her finish it," he said. "She has to."

Clarice arched backward, her eyes glowing gold and then silver. Her veins lit beneath her skin like burning rivers. Her breath caught—and then stopped.

Talon stepped forward at last—only to feel the change in the air before it arrived.

The emissary stepped from the far shadow.

Tall. Cloaked. His face hidden by a half-mask of etched silver. Rings gleamed on every finger—each one different. His voice, when he spoke, was a rasp of broken wind.

"She has awakened."

Talon raised his blade. "Stay where you are."

The emissary didn't move. "I came to see if the blood was truly hers. I see now it is."

Franco unsheathed a dagger. "Then you see your mistake."

The emissary laughed—soft, soulless.

"You cannot kill what is already ash."

And then he was gone—vanished in a burst of black vapor, leaving only the cold echo of his words behind.

Talon turned to Clarice. She lay still. Her pulse faint.

Franco dropped to his knees, pulling her into his arms. "Clarice. Clarice, stay with me."

Her eyes fluttered open. And they were silver.

Chapter 11: The Fire That Does Not Burn

Clarice's scream had faded into silence, but the ruins still echoed with its memory. Her body, now stilled, lay cradled in Franco's arms on the cold stones of Winchester Palace. The blood-vial had shattered beside her, the crimson remnants absorbed into the cracked earth like a seal broken and buried in ritual. Her chest rose with shallow, rhythmic breaths—unnatural, too even—and her skin shimmered faintly, like ash in moonlight.

Talon stood watch, sword still drawn, scanning the darkness at the ruin's edge. The emissary had vanished as suddenly as he appeared, leaving only tension in the air and a whisper that lingered: She has awakened.

Franco's eyes remained fixed on Clarice. "Her heart is steady," he murmured. "But her blood... it's different. I can feel it."

Talon finally turned, the blade at his side, his face unreadable. "Because she's no longer who she was. That vial wasn't a gift. It was a key."

Clarice stirred.

Her fingers twitched. Then her eyes opened—and where once they had been a stormy gray, they were now burnished silver, glowing softly like molten mirrors. She inhaled sharply and gasped, her body tensing as she sat upright. Franco steadied her, but she pulled from his arms.

"I remember," she said, her voice a shade deeper, echoing ever so slightly.

"Remember what?" Talon asked.

Clarice looked at her hands, turning them over in the moonlight. "My mother's final words. Not the ones she spoke aloud—but those she sealed inside the blood. Her last memory was of fire… and the thing beneath it."

Franco helped her to her feet. "Can you stand?"

She nodded slowly. "I'm not tired. I'm…" She hesitated, looking around the ruined palace. "I'm listening."

Talon narrowed his eyes. "To what?"

She turned to him. "To the blood of London. It speaks now. Every alley, every stone has a voice. I didn't hear them before. Now I can't stop."

For a long moment, Talon said nothing. Then he sheathed his blade. "You've crossed a threshold. And that means the Crownless will come harder. They'll see you not just as an heir… but as a weapon."

"I won't be theirs," Clarice said.

Franco placed a hand on her shoulder. "Then we protect you. And we use what you are to find what they're after."

Clarice nodded once. "I can do more than that."

She stepped to the center of the broken floor and knelt, placing her hand on the stone. Her fingers curled against it. She closed her eyes.

Franco and Talon stood silent as a pulse of silver light flickered beneath her palm—faint at first, then widening in a ripple that spread through the ruin like water beneath glass. The sigil carved into the floor by monks centuries ago glowed red, then violet, then black.

When Clarice opened her eyes again, her face was pale.

"They're beneath the city," she said. "In the Undervault. The old plague tunnels."

Talon's expression darkened. "No one's been there since the Black Death."

Franco's voice was grim. "That's where they've been building their court."

Clarice swayed slightly, and Franco caught her elbow.

"You're not ready for more tonight," he said gently.

She looked at him. "None of us are."

The following night, the house on Henrietta Street grew still.

Clarice slept, or appeared to. Franco had left her chamber only after she promised to rest. Now he stood at the hearth downstairs, staring into the flames. Talon poured two glasses of warmed bloodwine and handed one to him.

"You care for her," Talon said, his voice not accusatory, but measured.

"I care for all who are hunted," Franco replied, though his eyes did not meet Talon's. "You know that."

"She is not a girl anymore, Franco. She is something else now."

Franco finally turned. "And that frightens you."

Talon sipped from the glass, savoring the warmth. "No. It reminds me."

"Of what?"

"Of what I lost... when I believed in destiny instead of choice."

Franco stepped closer, reaching out to brush a hand along Talon's jaw. "You didn't lose me then. And you won't now."

Talon caught his hand and pressed it to his chest. "Then we face it together. Whatever's waiting in the dark."

Franco leaned in and kissed him. It was slow, deep, filled with memories and promises unspoken. When they parted, neither spoke. They simply stood in each other's arms, letting the fire warm the space between them.

———

By dawn, Talon had summoned allies.

Sir Lambert of the Old Kent Line arrived first—his coat stiff with dust, his eyes clouded by centuries, but still burning with loyalty. Behind him came Ysella, a bloodscribe from the Highland Clans, her mouth stained red with ink and prayer. Together, they formed the beginnings of a war council.

The map was unfurled again, and Clarice, pale but steady, traced her finger toward the ancient crypts beneath Borough.

"They're using plague catacombs as tunnels," she said. "They've carved a sanctum near the old Ossuary."

Sir Lambert scowled. "That place is cursed. Even the rats don't stay."

Talon nodded. "And yet that's where we'll go."

Clarice's voice was calm. "We don't have a choice."

Outside, the fog rolled heavier than before.

And in the cathedral tower nearest Temple Bar, the emissary stood in silence, his rings reflecting the morning light.

The silver flame had been lit.

And London would burn.

Chapter 12: The Storm Unleashed

The moon hung like a silent sentinel above the gathering, its pale light reflecting off the jagged edges of the ancient stone walls that surrounded the gardens. The night air was thick with the promise of something terrible—the kind of stillness that precedes a storm. Talon stood with his arms crossed, eyes narrowing as he watched the retreating forms of Ashford's emissaries slip back into the shadows. The confrontation had been brief, but its weight lingered in the air like the smell of old iron and rotted silk.

Franco stood beside him, his posture taut, hands gloved and still. The silence between them was not absence—it was anticipation. Around them, the faintest tremble rippled through the earth. London was awakening to something it had not seen in centuries.

"He's not finished," Franco murmured, his voice low. "He'll come again. And next time…"

"We'll be ready," Talon said.

Their eyes met, and no further words were needed.

They turned and walked in tandem toward the long stone corridor that led beneath the chapel ruins. Below, the others were waiting.

———

The war council had gathered in the vaulted crypt chamber beneath the city—a place that once held relics of the old Church, now stripped bare but for candlelight, weapons, and parchment. The round table, carved centuries earlier from black stone, bore the marks of other conflicts—scratches, scorch marks, grooves worn down by restless fingers.

Sir Lambert leaned over the table with both hands, a figure of weathered nobility. "The plague tunnels run from St. Giles to the Borough catacombs. If they're building sanctums beneath the Ossuary, they could breach the East Wing in a matter of days."

"They won't need days," said Ysella of the Highland Clans. She stood shrouded in her ink-black robes, her lips tinged with crimson rune powder. "Clarice's blood has already quickened them."

All heads turned toward Clarice.

She stood quietly at Talon's right, shoulders straight despite the fire in her veins. Her silver eyes caught the candlelight as if they were mirrors of it. She had changed, and none of them could deny it.

"I can feel them," she said softly. "Like a tide pushing against a dam. They've waited a long time. They'll wait no longer."

Franco placed a hand on her lower back. A small gesture. A grounding one. Talon's gaze flicked to it, and though he said nothing, the moment tightened something inside him.

"They want a war," Talon said. "Then we give them one. But on our ground."

Sir Lambert nodded. "We choke the tunnels. Collapse the arches. Force them into the open."

"They won't come alone," Ysella said. "The emissary is just the first. There are others. Shades. Revenants. Ashborne."

Clarice's voice cut through the room like a silver blade. "Then I go with you."

Talon turned sharply. "No."

She didn't flinch. "You need me. They're drawn to my blood. I can lead you to them."

"She's right," Franco said. "You know it."

Talon's jaw tightened. "I won't lose her."

"You won't," Clarice said. "But if I stay behind, we lose everything."

Silence fell again.

Then Talon exhaled slowly. "Then we go at dawn."

————

The sun never truly rose in London that day—only a grey dimness that bled through the fog, casting the buildings in a pallid wash of cold light. By twilight, they stood gathered at the old entrance to the plague tunnels—a crumbling archway beneath the ruins of a shuttered tannery near Southwark. The air reeked of old leather and salt, but beneath that... something older. A coppery tang of rot and centuries-old death.

Clarice took the lead, flanked by Franco and Ysella. Talon brought up the rear, his sword already drawn.

The tunnels were narrow at first—barely shoulder-width, winding like intestines beneath the skin of the city. The walls dripped with condensation, and every step sent echoes through the stone like whispers in a crypt. They passed piles of forgotten debris: lanterns, broken teeth, a child's doll speckled in mildew.

They had walked a mile when they reached the Ossuary.

It was vast.

Bones lined the walls in stacked spirals—skulls staring outward in silent warning. Some still bore the etchings of plague wards. Others were cracked clean through. In the center, a great dais rose—stone carved in runes none of them could read.

Talon stepped forward and crouched beside one of the bones. "These aren't all human."

Ysella ran her fingers along the runes. "This is where they've anchored their court."

Clarice moved ahead, her hand trembling slightly. The magic was stronger here. It buzzed in her blood, pulled her toward something unseen.

Then she stopped.

At the far end of the chamber stood a man.

Or something that wore the shape of one.

He was tall, draped in black stitched with silver thread. His hands bore the rings—the emissary. His mask gleamed in the torchlight, etched with symbols that seemed to move when one stared too long.

"You brought her," he said.

Talon stepped between them, sword raised. "You won't touch her."

The emissary tilted his head. "We do not wish to touch her. Only to receive what is ours."

Clarice stepped forward. "I am not yours."

He turned to her. "But you are. You carry our inheritance. That which was taken from us in fire. Your blood is the seal and the key. When you bleed, the gate opens."

She lifted her hand.

And the flames erupted.

Silver fire spiraled from her palm, bright as moonlight, crashing into the emissary with a force that cracked the bones in the wall. He staggered back, his mask fractured, revealing a glimpse of pale, eyeless skin beneath.

Talon was beside her in an instant.

"Now!" he shouted.

Franco and Sir Lambert charged, blades raised, Ysella chanting in tongues older than English. The battle raged beneath the city, magic and metal colliding in a storm of shrieks and echoing roars. The emissary howled—not in pain, but in fury.

"I will return," he hissed before vanishing in a cloud of black ash.

And then there was silence.

Only the breath of the living and the hum of the newly awakened.

Clarice stood in the aftermath, her eyes still glowing, her hand still burning faintly with fire. Franco touched her cheek.

"You did it," he whispered.

"No," she said. "We've only opened the door."

Talon looked toward the bones, the runes, the darkness beyond.

"They're coming now," he said.

And from far below, something stirred.

Chapter 13: The Gathering Storm

The Ossuary stank of blood and smoke. The runes etched into the bone walls still glowed faintly from Clarice's fire, the silver sparks seared into the silence like constellations carved by war. But the emissary was gone, and with him, the last fragile thread of secrecy that had held back the tide. Now, every clan would know.

Talon stood amid the ruin, his blade still humming faintly from its last clash. Across the chamber, Franco knelt beside Clarice, wiping soot from her cheek with the corner of his sleeve. Her eyes had dimmed to a silvery gray, but the light of something older still pulsed beneath her skin. A lock had turned in her soul. The door had opened.

"They'll come now," Talon said. "The Crownless. All of them."

Clarice slowly stood. "Then we meet them."

"No," Talon snapped, spinning toward her. "You did your part. You awakened what was needed. The rest is ours."

She didn't flinch. "You think they'll stop if I stand aside?"

"No," Franco said gently. "But we're not sending you to the front lines either."

"I'm not a relic," she replied, stepping forward. "And I'm not your charge."

Franco held up a hand. "We know. But we've fought these things before. We know what it costs."

Clarice turned her eyes on Talon, challenging, defiant. "And what have you lost, Talon, that makes you so eager to bleed for me, yet so unwilling to let me do the same?"

Talon's expression flickered. "Everything," he said quietly. "I've lost everything. And I won't lose again."

For a moment, the room was deathly still. Only the soft crackle of residual magic filled the silence. Then Franco moved between them.

"We need to return," he said. "Tonight."

Talon nodded, not trusting himself to speak.

————

Back in the crypt beneath St. Bride's, the vampire court had already begun to splinter.

The table was crowded now—clan elders and blood chancellors from across London packed the chamber with voices sharp as daggers and eyes gleaming with suspicion. At the head, Talon stood flanked by Franco and Clarice, facing the storm.

"You led her to the Ossuary," barked Lord Mortimer of Shadowfang, his crimson cloak sweeping the stones like smoke. "You lit the fire that wakes the dead!"

"Because they were already coming," Franco answered coolly. "We didn't strike the match. We revealed the fuse."

"Semantics!" Mortimer spat. "And who do we name when the tunnels collapse and blood rains on Whitehall?"

Clarice stepped forward. "Name me. I'll wear it."

Gasps echoed through the room. Talon didn't look at her, but his jaw flexed.

"Bold," murmured Lady Seraphina of Bloodthorn. "But boldness does not win wars. Strategy does."

Ysella of the Highland Clans raised her voice then, calm and clear. "The fire has started. There's no snuffing it now. We choose our ground or they choose it for us."

Talon laid his hands flat on the table. "We stand at Valewind Pass. We control the high ground. We collapse the tunnels behind us and draw them to the surface."

"Valewind is cursed," someone muttered.

"It's perfect," Talon said. "No clan claims it. No bloodline is sovereign there. Only the earth itself. And the earth remembers."

Franco looked across the table. "If any of you want to survive, follow us. If not—stay and rot beneath your estates."

There was silence.

Then Sir Lambert rose and nodded once. "Valewind."

One by one, others joined him. Not all. But enough.

———

That night, Talon stood in the library alone, pouring over maps and old texts by candlelight. Rain battered the windows. The storm outside mirrored the one within. When Franco entered, Talon didn't look up.

"She shouldn't have spoken like that in the council," Talon said.

Franco approached him slowly. "You mean she shouldn't have stolen your thunder?"

Talon looked up, blue eyes hard. "She's still learning what she is. Power like that—"

"—needs to be wielded or it eats you alive," Franco finished. "I know."

They stood quietly, the shadows long around them.

Talon finally broke. "You believe in her."

"I believe in both of you," Franco said. "And I'm tired of being the only one who believes in me."

Talon moved closer then, stepping into his space, wrapping a hand around the back of Franco's neck. Their kiss was slow and bruising, laced with grief and need. Talon pulled him in until their foreheads touched, breath mingling.

"I don't want to lose you," he whispered.

"You won't," Franco replied.

"But if I do," Talon said, voice cracking, "this world won't survive me."

———

In her chamber, Clarice stood alone before the mirror. Her reflection had begun to blur at the edges. She was no longer entirely mortal. Her heartbeat came slower. Her skin had taken on a faint iridescence. And behind her eyes… were shadows of things not yet seen.

On her windowsill, the wind rattled the panes.

Far across the city, in the catacombs beneath Westminster, the emissary knelt before a throne of bone.

"She has awakened," he said.

A figure in a silver shroud stirred upon the throne.

"Then so shall we."

And the dead began to rise.

Chapter 14: Valewind Pass

The wind that blew across Valewind was ancient, carved from the bones of forgotten kings and soaked in the whispers of war. The land itself remembered. It groaned beneath footfalls, its narrow ridge cut between two sheer drops—one into the wood-choked basin of Shadowmere, the other into a ravine long swallowed by ash. No flags flew there, no monuments stood. Just bare stone, pocked by old fire and the weight of old death.

It was the perfect place to bleed.

Talon stood atop the rise where the pass narrowed into a throat, his cloak sweeping in the wind. The map of the terrain had been burned into his memory the moment he first walked it centuries ago. He had bled here once, a decade before Franco. Long before he learned that immortality carried the loneliness of legacy.

Behind him, the sound of boots echoed—an army arriving not as one, but in waves.

Franco approached first, his dark hair tousled by the wind, his coat stained with dust and readiness. "Moonveil has arrived," he said, stopping beside Talon. "Sir Cedric rides at the front with fifty bloodborn archers. Ironroot comes behind them with a wall of shields. Frostspire is still a half day out, but they're coming."

"And the Highland Clans?" Talon asked.

Franco's voice darkened. "Still silent."

Talon's mouth curled into a bitter line. "Cowards dressed in ghosts."

"No," Franco said. "They're waiting to see if we survive."

Talon didn't reply. He watched the fog rolling in over the lowlands—thick and slow, carrying with it a scent he recognized. Earth. Decay. Magic older than scripture.

"We make our stand here," he said. "We hold the pass. If they push through, there's nothing to stop them from reaching the heart of the city."

Franco looked out with him. "Then they don't get through."

———

They pitched their forward command within the ruins of a fallen tower on the ridge, its roof long gone, ivy overtaking the broken walls like veins reclaiming a corpse. By nightfall, the old stone chamber was lit with lanterns, and a war council gathered within.

Sir Cedric of Moonveil—tall, gaunt, eyes ringed with centuries—leaned over the battle map, his fingers tracing the line of the pass. "We build a barricade here. Ironroot plants the shieldwall. Your archers rain hell from the upper ridge. But if they breach it—"

"They won't," Franco said.

Ysella stood across from him, robed in black, her hands stained with ink and fresh blood. "You can't hold against what you don't understand. The Crownless don't march like armies. They pour. Like fire. Like rot."

"We meet them with fire of our own," Clarice said from the shadow of the wall.

The others turned as she stepped into the light. Her silver eyes caught the flame. She no longer walked like a girl unsure of her footing. She moved with silence and purpose—like prophecy given flesh.

"I can see where they'll come," she continued. "They'll use the ridge path and the old tunnels beneath the pass. If they've corrupted the bone paths under the mountain, they'll rise behind us."

Talon stepped to her side. "You'll lead the second guard. If they breach the inner line, you burn it shut."

She met his gaze, unwavering. "I'll hold it."

Franco's voice was softer. "Not alone."

Clarice turned to him, lips twitching into the barest smile. "I know. That's why you'll be with me."

———

As night fell, the wind turned colder, carrying with it a stillness that wasn't peace, but the deep inhalation before the scream.

In their tent, Franco sat sharpening a dagger, his thoughts restless. Talon stood behind him, silent.

"You haven't said what you're thinking," Franco said at last.

Talon moved to sit beside him. "I'm thinking we've lived through nearly three centuries and are somehow still standing in dirt, drawing battle lines in blood."

Franco's smile was faint. "We've always stood in blood."

Talon reached out, his hand brushing along Franco's jaw. "But never like this. This feels different."

Franco looked at him, eyes unreadable. "Because we care about what comes after."

They were silent for a moment, and then Talon kissed him —soft at first, then deeper, hungrier. Their bond had always been their salvation. It grounded Talon when the world begged for war and reminded Franco that there was still something worth surviving for.

When they parted, Franco whispered, "If we don't make it —"

"We will," Talon interrupted.

"If we don't," Franco continued, "I want you to remember this. This moment. Not the sword. Not the war. Just this."

Talon didn't answer. He didn't need to.

———

At midnight, the sentries lit the ridge torches. Clarice stood in her cloak of black and silver, her fingers twitching as the magic pulsed through her. Ysella painted protective runes across the entrance to the tunnel, whispering to the old gods as she worked.

The scouts returned before dawn.

And their message was brief.

"They come."

Talon stood on the ridge as the first shapes emerged from the fog—dozens, then hundreds, cloaked in shadow, some dragging weapons carved from bone, others barefoot and silent. Their faces were pale and smooth, their mouths split too wide, and their eyes glowed faint silver.

And at the front, taller than the rest, a figure in silver robes and a crown of thorns stepped forward.

The High Lord of the Crownless Court.

He raised one hand.

And the storm began.

Chapter 15: Valewind Ignites

At first, there was only silence. The kind that wraps the earth before a thunderstorm—when birds vanish, trees stiffen, and even the wind forgets how to move.

Talon stood at the mouth of Valewind Pass, his cloak billowing against the narrow ridge wind, sword gripped in a gauntlet of black leather. The moon loomed like a sentinel, bright and merciless. Behind him stretched the gathered force of their alliance—Moonveil's archers stationed atop crags, Ironroot's shieldwall planted along the center path, and the quick-strike spearmen of Frostspire crouched like silver-scaled serpents in the flanks of the slope. Clarice stood cloaked in black, her fingertips glowing with soft silver light, and Franco was at her side, his blades already drawn.

Across the valley, the Crownless Court arrived.

They came not as men, nor as an army. They came as a plague.

Figures poured from the mouth of the low tunnels, robed in bone-pale fabric that fluttered like skin. Their movements were wrong—gliding instead of walking, their limbs bending at angles that defied bone. Their faces were featureless masks of white, lips sealed, eyes black pits, and yet they moved in perfect, silent unity.

At the center of them stood the crowned one.

He was tall, wrapped in robes of tarnished silver and lined with scars that glowed like molten veins. His face was veiled, but the crown of thorns atop his brow pulsed like it was alive, vines of black iron twisting down into his flesh.

Talon stepped forward, raising his sword.

"You are not welcome here," he called.

The crowned one did not speak. He raised his hand, and the mask-faced things around him stopped—then dropped to the ground like shadows melting into stone.

Clarice stiffened. "He's summoning them."

Franco narrowed his eyes. "What are they—"

From the ground, the creatures began to rise again—but different.

Transformed.

Their limbs extended, twisting into hooked claws. Their mouths tore open with the sound of wet silk, revealing rows of jagged teeth. Their robes burned away, revealing bodies made of tendons and bone and black, smoking veins.

Clarice whispered, "These aren't just vampires."

"No," Talon said. "They're revenants. Made, not born."

The crowned one lowered his hand.

And the horde charged.

———

The first wave hit Ironroot's shieldwall like a tidal wave of meat and claw. Shields splintered under impact, steel screamed against bone, and the air filled with a roar not of voices but of wind forced through shattered mouths. Sir Cedric's archers loosed a volley from above—silver-tipped arrows raining like ice—but even those that fell rose again, crawling forward on broken limbs.

Talon and Franco were already moving.

Franco vanished into the left flank, blades flashing in arcs of silver, his movements a dance of death and control. Talon plunged into the heart of the melee, his black blade gleaming with runes as it met flesh and shadow. With each strike, he carved down another revenant, his face calm, almost still, as if he were walking through memory.

On the ridge, Clarice knelt, eyes closed. Her palms pressed to the earth.

"They're using blood lines," she whispered to herself. "Old tunnels. They'll breach from below."

Ysella stood behind her, chanting in a low voice, blood trailing from her fingertips into runes drawn into the stone. "Then stop them, child. Stop them before they rot the bones of the pass."

Clarice opened her eyes, glowing now with radiant silver. "I need more."

"You'll take it," Ysella said, "or we all die."

Clarice screamed—loud and sharp, not of pain, but release. Silver fire exploded from her hands and streaked through the runes. The ground beneath the battlefield cracked.

From the depths, shrieks echoed. The second wave had been rising.

She burned them alive before they could surface.

The earth trembled.

———

Talon turned in time to see Clarice's fire consume the tunnel mouths. He felt the heat across the ridge and saw the flickering outlines of blackened figures falling back into the crevice. His chest clenched—not in fear, but in awe.

Then the crowned one moved.

With slow, regal grace, he descended the field, untouched by the chaos around him. As he passed, the revenants parted, bowing their malformed bodies in eerie reverence.

Talon stepped forward. Franco appeared at his side.

The air between them shimmered.

"You," Talon said, pointing his blade. "No more messengers. No more masks. Just you and me."

The crowned one's voice filled the air—low, echoing from every direction. "You do not understand, Talon. You are not fighting me. You are fighting time."

Franco narrowed his eyes. "Then let's run out the clock."

The crowned one raised a hand, and the crown of thorns upon his brow expanded, its vines stretching, twisting toward the ground.

Clarice stepped between them.

"No," she said. "This ends with me."

The crowned one paused.

"You would claim your inheritance?" he asked.

"I'd burn it," Clarice replied, "before I let you wear it."

She raised both hands.

The silver fire roared.

It met the crowned one's vines mid-air and exploded in a shockwave that leveled the front ranks of both armies. Talon and Franco shielded their faces as magic screamed past them. The crowned one staggered—just slightly—and let out a sound between a laugh and a snarl.

"She's more than we feared," he hissed.

"And less than you hoped," Talon said—and charged.

The battle between Talon and the crowned one was thunder without sound. Their blades met in flashes of lightning, curses burned into the earth beneath their feet. Franco fought beside him, shielding his flank, his own blades slick with the black ichor of revenants.

Clarice's fire held the rear.

But they were outnumbered. Even with her magic, even with the wall.

It wouldn't be enough.

Until the horns blew.

High and clear, from the northern ridge.

Talon looked up in disbelief.

From the trees, banners emerged.

The Highland Clans had come.

Ysella raised her arms in prayer. "At last."

The tide turned.

And the pass, once a place of silence and ash, roared with fire, war, and the cries of the undead as they began—finally—to die.

Chapter 16: Ash Beneath the Skin

The wind over Valewind Pass was quiet again.

Where screams and fire had roared only hours before, silence now hung heavy—broken only by the crackle of dying torches and the moaning of wounded fighters scattered across the slope. The bodies of the Crownless revenants burned where they fell, releasing smoke that curled unnaturally against the breeze, refusing to dissipate.

Talon stood at the highest ridge, blood still drying on his sword. His cloak was torn, the left shoulder of his coat soaked crimson. But he didn't feel the pain—not yet. All he felt was the weight of what had been lost.

Sir Lambert was dead. Half of Ironroot's shield wall gone with him. The Frostspire spearmen had shattered under the second wave, and while the Highland Clans had turned the tide, they'd arrived only after the valley drank deeply of blood.

Clarice's silver fire had done more than defend them. It had scorched a chasm into the earth itself. The pass would never be the same.

Behind him, Franco stood with his hands on his knees, breath catching raggedly in his chest. His swords were dark with ichor, his face pale beneath a mask of ash. Clarice leaned against a broken pillar, silver still glowing faintly beneath her skin. Her eyes were wide—not with fear, but with what she had done.

"What now?" she asked softly.

Talon turned. His face was unreadable.

"Now we bury our dead."

———

The war camp had been moved just beyond the southern rise, hidden by rocks and hawthorn trees. Medical tents sprang up overnight. Vampires rarely required healing in the traditional sense, but silver wounds, enchanted strikes, and trauma needed time. Some warriors would not rise again—not because they were destroyed, but because they had seen too much.

Franco sat on a low bench beside Clarice, watching her hands tremble as she reached for a flask of water.

"You're still burning," he said.

"I know." Her voice was brittle.

He placed a hand gently over hers. "You held back."

She didn't deny it. "If I had let it all go… I don't know who I would've become."

Their eyes met.

Franco said nothing, but his hand didn't move.

Talon watched them from across the tent. He hadn't spoken much since the fighting stopped. Not to Franco. Not to Clarice. Not even to the surviving clan leaders.

He turned and left without a word.

———

Talon stood alone near the edge of the ravine where the enemy first emerged. The earth here was scorched, blackened bones still caught in the roots of the soil. He stared into the void, jaw clenched.

He didn't hear Franco approach.

"You've barely spoken," Franco said.

"There's nothing left to say," Talon replied.

Franco stepped beside him. "Don't do that."

"Do what?"

"Shut me out."

Talon finally looked at him, and there was something in his eyes that Franco hadn't seen in decades—uncertainty.

"You didn't see her," Talon said. "When she burned the ground beneath them. That wasn't control. That was instinct."

"She saved us."

Talon nodded slowly. "Yes. But I don't think she knows what she's becoming."

Franco folded his arms. "You're afraid of her."

"I'm afraid of losing you to her," Talon said quietly. "And I hate myself for it."

Franco was silent.

"I see the way you look at her," Talon added.

"She's not a wedge between us," Franco said. "Unless we let her be."

Talon turned away, staring into the dark. "You're slipping away, Franco. I feel it. And I don't know how to stop it."

"You can't stop change, Talon," Franco said. "You taught me that."

And with that, he walked back toward the camp, leaving Talon alone beneath the gray sky.

Clarice wandered beyond the tents that night, toward a patch of unmarked graves. She stood between two wooden posts hammered into the ground, eyes fixed on the pale moon.

Franco found her there.

"They're afraid of me now," she said softly.

"They're afraid of what they don't understand."

"I'm afraid of it too," she whispered. "I felt something during the battle... something pull me deeper. If I had gone with it, I don't know if I'd have stopped."

Franco placed a hand on her back. "But you did."

Clarice turned to him. "Do you hate me for what I'm doing to him?"

"No," Franco said. "But I think he might hate himself for not knowing how to stop it."

She stepped closer. "You love him."

"I always will."

"And yet..."

Franco didn't answer.

She leaned her forehead against his shoulder. He didn't move away.

Somewhere behind them, Talon watched.

And turned away.

———

Far below the ruins of Valewind, the Crownless Court stirred again.

The crowned one stood before a circle of ash and whispered, "They are fractured."

From the shadow, a voice answered: "Then we break them."

And the war, far from over, began its second act.

Chapter 17: The Silence Between

The embers of Valewind still glowed behind their eyes.

Though days had passed since the battle, the air over the war camp remained thick, pressed down by the grief that lingers in the wake of slaughter. The survivors moved like shadows—tending the wounded, burying the dead, sharpening blades in silence. It was not victory they felt. It was delay. The kind of hush that knew another storm was coming, only worse.

Talon had not returned to the council tent. He spent his nights on the ridge alone, a black silhouette against the dull gray dawn, barely speaking, barely sleeping. His silence was a kind of mourning, but also something else—retreat.

Franco watched from afar.

He had tried, more than once, to reach him. But Talon gave him only fragments: a glance, a nod, a word. The weight between them was not blame. It was the ache of love standing too close to change.

Clarice hadn't spoken to either of them beyond necessity. She spent her hours with Ysella, practicing restraint. Learning to call the fire without letting it burn her from the inside out.

But even Ysella saw it: Clarice's center had shifted. She was no longer a girl resisting her birthright. She was becoming something else.

She's not just the key anymore, Ysella had said to Franco. She is the door itself.

———

Talon stood beneath the twisted boughs of a dead tree on the southern cliff. Below, the charred remnants of revenants still blackened the rocks.

He heard Franco approach before he spoke.

"You haven't been sleeping," Franco said.

Talon didn't turn. "I don't sleep anymore."

"You used to."

Talon was silent for a long time.

Then: "I dream of her fire."

Franco stepped beside him. "You think it will consume her?"

Talon's jaw tightened. "I think it already is."

Franco exhaled slowly. "And if she controls it?"

"She won't." Talon turned at last. His eyes were darker than usual. "Not forever."

Franco searched his face. "Is that fear speaking—or jealousy?"

Talon blinked, but didn't deny it.

Franco's voice lowered. "I don't love her like I love you."

"But you do love her," Talon said.

Franco looked away. "Not yet."

Talon nodded once. "But you will."

The silence between them was heavier than any blade.

Then Talon stepped back. "She needs you more than I do."

Franco's voice was quiet. "Do you believe that?"

"No," Talon said. "But I think you do."

———

Clarice sat cross-legged in the center of a ruined chapel, the bones of the ceiling long since collapsed, open to the sky above. Silver fire danced faintly between her fingers, small now, controlled. A soft hum echoed from the runes Ysella had carved around her.

Franco watched her from the archway.

She opened her eyes. "You're staring."

He smiled faintly. "Impressed. Maybe worried."

She looked back at the fire in her palm. "It's louder now. Not painful. Just... constant. Like a voice behind the wall, whispering names I don't know."

Franco stepped closer. "You're stronger every day."

She let the flame die out. "It's not strength, Franco. It's unraveling."

He knelt beside her. "You're not alone."

Her eyes met his. "Aren't I?"

They stayed like that—too close, too quiet.

Then Clarice looked away. "He's slipping from you."

Franco's breath caught. "I know."

"I didn't mean to cause it."

"I don't think you did."

She hesitated. "But?"

Franco exhaled. "But he sees it anyway."

Clarice rested her hand on his. "If this ends badly... I don't want it to be because we lied to each other."

Franco's voice was soft. "We haven't. Not yet."

Behind them, Ysella watched from the shadows, her ink-stained hands clenched at her sides.

"The moment you hesitate," she whispered, "he'll take her."

———

Elsewhere, deep in the buried catacombs beneath Shoreditch, the Crownless Court gathered again.

The crowned one stood at the altar of bone, surrounded by his inner circle—creatures who no longer remembered what warmth felt like. The emissary knelt, his mask cracked, the silver rings on his fingers smeared with dried blood.

"She is ascending," the emissary said.

"Then the time is now," the crowned one replied. "We strike not at the pass—but at the heart."

A new voice echoed through the chamber—low, velvet, and terrifying.

"Then let me go to them."

A figure stepped forward from the dark—a woman cloaked in midnight and feathers, her eyes bright as polished obsidian.

The crowned one inclined his head. "Ah. The Whisperer's heir."

She smiled, and it was not kind. "Let me unmake what the fire has shaped."

The emissary bowed lower.

"She will never see it coming."

———

That night, Talon returned to camp at last.

He entered the council tent and sat in silence as Ysella and Sir Cedric debated fortification plans. Franco watched him the entire time, but Talon's gaze never rose.

Later, Clarice found him alone in the ruins of the old tower.

"You haven't looked at me in days," she said.

He didn't move. "I see you more clearly than ever."

She stepped closer. "Do you hate me?"

"No," he said. "I envy you."

She blinked. "Why?"

"Because he follows you now."

Clarice's voice was barely a whisper. "That's not my fault."

"No," Talon said, eyes locked on the dying fire. "But it will be my loss."

And far below, the Crownless prepared their next strike.

Not on Valewind.

But into the heart of the alliance itself.

Chapter 18: The Fracture That Burns

The sky above the camp was black, not with night, but with smoke. Fires flickered at the northern edge—controlled burns to ward off revenants, Ysella said—but to Talon, it felt like a warning. A funeral pyre yet to be named.

Clarice stood in the center of the warded circle Ysella had carved the night before. The silver dust that protected it had begun to dull, its shimmer absorbed by the earth, drained by something unseen. The rune-sigil pulsed weakly, then faltered.

"It's decaying," she said. "The wards are fading faster now."

Ysella crouched beside her. "Because something stronger is approaching."

Clarice turned, the wind pulling at her cloak. "Not stronger. Colder."

Franco entered then, his sword strapped across his back, his sleeves rolled to the elbows. He looked tired. Not wounded—but worn down by a battle that hadn't yet begun.

"We may have a breach on the eastern trail," he said. "Scouts are reporting missing sentries."

Talon stepped in just behind him, arms folded. "You think it's them?"

Franco turned. "Who else would it be?"

There was a beat of silence between them. Not hostile. But no longer familiar.

Talon looked at Clarice. "Don't leave the circle."

"I can help," she said.

Talon's voice was sharper than intended. "You can burn through a mountain, but you haven't learned how to contain yourself. We don't need a flare. We need precision."

Franco looked between them, brow furrowed.

Clarice said nothing. But the silver at her temples flared—just slightly.

She was holding back. But not for much longer.

———

They found the body at dusk.

The sentry was pinned to a tree with a dagger of black bone. His throat torn. His eyes wide. No blood—only a message carved across his chest in a language Talon hadn't seen in three hundred years.

"It's old," he muttered. "Northern crypt script. Crownless dialect."

"What does it say?" Franco asked.

Talon didn't answer right away. Then: "Inheritance burns."

They stood in silence.

Franco turned to the woods. "They're provoking her."

"Yes," Talon said. "And they know how."

Franco looked at him. "You're not being fair to her."

"I'm trying to keep her alive," Talon snapped. "You, too."

"You're not keeping us alive, Talon," Franco replied. "You're keeping us apart."

———

That night, Clarice left her tent.

She walked alone into the ruins beyond the camp, the ash crunching beneath her boots, the silver flicker in her eyes faint but steady. She didn't mean to find Franco there.

But she did.

He was sitting on a broken column, his cloak draped beside him, hands buried in his hair. He didn't look up.

She didn't speak. She just sat beside him.

"I tried to talk to him," Franco said after a while. "But it's like... it's like I don't know how anymore."

Clarice turned to him. "He loves you."

"I know."

"But you're changing."

Franco's voice was soft. "So are you."

She reached out, brushing a bit of soot from his cheek. "I didn't ask for any of this."

"No," Franco said. "But neither did he."

She let her hand fall. "Do you think there's a version of this where we all survive?"

"I used to."

He looked at her. And there, in the shattered shadow of war and starlight, they didn't kiss.

But they thought about it.

And it was almost worse.

———

The Crownless Court struck just before dawn.

Not with force.

But with horror.

The firewatch at the eastern barricade lit a beacon—and then screamed. Not a cry of pain. But a single, long, soul-ripping scream that didn't stop.

When Talon arrived, he found the sentries alive—every one of them.

But blind.

Their eyes were burned white. Their hands trembled. And every one of them whispered the same phrase: "She belongs to us."

Talon stumbled back from the last soldier, breath ragged. Franco appeared behind him.

"They didn't kill anyone," he said.

"No," Talon murmured. "They're breaking the seams."

———

Later that morning, in the council tent, Talon stood before the gathered leaders.

"We strike now," he said. "We don't wait for another message. We don't let them inside our walls again."

Ysella raised a hand. "We're not ready."

"We'll never be ready," he replied.

Clarice entered then. The room shifted.

She walked to the center of the war table and laid down the map Ysella had drawn days before. The sigils were now blackened. Every ward they had placed had failed.

"They've found a way to poison our protections," Clarice said. "They're inside our wards. But they're not using brute force."

"They're using fear," Talon said.

She turned to him. "And it's working."

The room emptied after the meeting, but Talon didn't leave.

Neither did she.

"You need to tell him," she said.

Talon raised an eyebrow. "Tell him what?"

"That you're letting him go."

The words cut sharper than any blade.

He said nothing.

"You love him," Clarice whispered. "But you're already stepping back."

Talon looked away. "You don't know what you're talking about."

"I know exactly what it feels like to hold something you were never meant to keep."

Talon met her gaze. "Then you know it hurts."

She didn't blink. "So make it mean something."

Outside, the wind howled.

And in the deep hollow beneath the earth, the Crownless Court smiled.

They had cracked the bond.

Now they would shatter it.

Chapter 19: The Blade Between

The fog that rolled into the camp before dawn was not the natural kind. It clung to the skin, not with moisture, but with memory—each breath carried the scent of blood long spilled, of promises once whispered and broken beneath moonlight.

Talon stood alone outside the command tent, cloak drawn tight, boots rooted to frost-kissed earth. The silence between him and Franco had become something with weight. Something that moved through the camp like a rumor too painful to name.

Clarice had not spoken since the sentries were blinded. She trained. She burned. She stood in the rune circle every day until her nose bled and her fingertips smoked.

And still, the Court came closer.

———

The scout's body was found at the river bend just after sunrise—mouth sewn shut with silver thread, eyes plucked clean, limbs twisted like he had tried to escape his own skin. Across his chest was branded the same phrase as before, this time in deeper cuts: She was ours first.

Ysella knelt beside the corpse, her face like marble.

"They're no longer trying to frighten her," she said. "They're trying to claim her."

Franco arrived moments later. When he saw the body, his shoulders stiffened.

Talon watched him from a distance.

He knew what was coming. Not from the Court. From within.

———

In the council tent that night, the maps remained unrolled, but no one studied them.

"We're losing the perimeter," said Sir Cedric. "The Court has taken every eastern path. They're carving a circle around us."

"They want us to run," Clarice said. "They want to watch us scatter."

"No," Talon replied. "They want to break us first."

He looked at Franco. "They're doing it."

Franco's gaze didn't meet his. "Then we have to strike first."

Silence.

Talon turned to the table, hands pressed flat against the stone. "Tomorrow, we descend into the tunnels beneath the Eastern Graves. It's the last route not yet sealed."

Clarice's voice was cold. "A trap."

"Yes," Talon said. "But it's our trap. We set the rules."

———

That night, the argument happened not in war tents or graveyards—but beneath the stars.

Talon sat sharpening his sword near the ruined chapel, the blade whispering against whetstone. Franco approached, arms folded, jaw tight.

"You don't speak to me anymore," Franco said.

"You don't want to hear what I have to say," Talon replied.

Franco's voice hardened. "Try me."

Talon paused. "You're in love with her."

Franco blinked, as if slapped.

"That's not fair," he said.

"Isn't it?" Talon's eyes were bright with a kind of agony. "I've felt you slipping, Franco. For months now. I watched you fall in love and pretend it wasn't happening."

Franco stepped forward. "I never lied to you."

"No," Talon whispered. "But you left me behind anyway."

The silence between them hurt more than any blade.

And from the woods, Clarice stood watching—unseen, but not untouched.

———

They descended into the Eastern Graves the next day with two dozen warriors—Talon at the front, Franco at his side, Clarice behind them, silent as frost. The tunnels beneath the graveyard were lined with broken coffins, half-eaten bones, and old sacrificial rings. Every step echoed like a heartbeat.

They did not see the ambush until it was too late.

The Crownless came from the walls—emerging from the stone like smoke. Dozens of them. Silent. Smiling.

The emissary appeared last, silver rings dripping black blood.

"Welcome home," he said.

Talon and Franco fell into position instantly, blades raised.

Clarice's eyes flared silver.

But the Court wasn't attacking her.

They surrounded Talon.

Franco moved to protect him—but Clarice stepped forward, hand raised.

"They're not here to kill," she said. "They're here to choose."

And then it happened.

From the shadows, stepped her.

The woman with obsidian eyes.

The Whisperer's heir.

She looked like Clarice—only older, darker, worn hollow by time and power.

"Hello, sister," she said.

Clarice froze.

"You took what was mine," the woman said. "You wear the flame, but it was meant for me."

Franco stepped between them. "Who are you?"

The woman's gaze flicked to him. "Someone she forgot."

Talon watched Clarice carefully. Her hands trembled.

The woman raised a hand—and the revenants charged.

The battle was chaos. Fire against shadow. Talon's blade sang, Franco's daggers flashing like lightning. Clarice unleashed a wave of light so fierce it blinded even the Crownless, but it was too late.

They had breached the lines.

They had learned.

And they had taken someone.

When the smoke cleared, the emissary was gone.

And so was Clarice.

————

Franco searched the battlefield like a man possessed. Tore through corpses. Screamed her name into the darkness. Ignored the blood soaking his coat, the wounds down his arms.

Talon watched from the edge of the carnage, silent.

When Franco finally turned to him, eyes wild with grief, he said only one thing:

"We have to get her back."

Talon's voice was hollow. "Even if she chose to go?"

Franco's face twisted. "Don't say that."

"She stood still," Talon said. "She let them come."

Franco staggered back as if struck.

"You don't believe that," he whispered.

Talon turned away. "I don't know what I believe anymore."

And for the first time in centuries—

They didn't stand together.

They stood apart.

———

Beneath the earth, Clarice awoke.

Chained.

Surrounded by ash.

And her sister smiled beside her.

"Now," the woman said, brushing Clarice's hair from her face, "let me show you what real inheritance feels like."

Chapter 20: The Chains of Inheritance

The catacombs beneath Shoreditch were not carved—they were grown. Long tunnels of root-tangled stone ran like veins beneath the graveyards, expanding with each century, each death, each secret no one dared speak aloud. And in their deepest chamber, where no light could reach, Clarice awoke.

She lay on a cold slab of petrified bone, her wrists chained above her head, the metal infused with salt and bloodbinding runes. Her body ached, not from pain, but from restraint. The fire in her veins swirled, furious, unable to burn.

Across the room, her sister watched.

"You sleep like a mortal," the woman said, voice low and melodic. "But you are not."

Clarice raised her head slowly. "You're not my sister."

The woman stepped forward. Her dark cloak dragged across the stone. Her features were like Clarice's—if one stripped away every softness, every kindness. Where Clarice's eyes shimmered silver, hers were coal-black, and burned with nothing but hunger.

"We were born of the same line," she said. "My name is Nerya. Daughter of the first Whisperer. Your mother was a branch. I am the root."

Clarice's chains rattled as she shifted. "You betrayed your own blood."

"No." Nerya smiled. "I claimed it."

She raised a hand, and the silver flame ignited within Clarice's chest—without her will. Clarice gasped, her body arching as the magic pulsed through her veins like molten lightning.

Nerya watched her writhe. "They taught you to fear it. Talon. Ysella. Even Franco, though he hides it well. But I will teach you to own it."

Clarice's breath was ragged. "You'll break me before I ever become like you."

Nerya tilted her head. "Darling, you're already becoming me."

————

Above ground, the air at camp was brittle.

Franco stood at the edge of the last known entrance to the catacombs, staring down into the dark like it might speak Clarice's name. His jaw was clenched, eyes bloodshot from lack of sleep. He hadn't eaten. Had barcly spoken.

Talon watched him from a distance.

He'd stopped trying to reach out two days ago.

Every time he tried, he could feel the wall between them thicken—poured from shared guilt, from something deeper than heartbreak. They still fought together, planned together—but not like before.

Now it was duty, not love.

He found Franco later that night sharpening his blade alone, near the hollow of the chapel ruins.

"She's still alive," Talon said.

Franco didn't look up. "You don't know that."

"I feel it."

Franco stood, pacing. "Then why aren't we doing anything?"

"Because we don't know where she is."

Franco spun. "We know enough."

Talon's voice was low. "You're not thinking clearly."

"No," Franco said, stepping closer. "I'm thinking like someone who still believes she's worth saving."

Talon flinched, just slightly.

Franco's expression faltered. "That's not what I meant—"

"But it's what you said," Talon cut in, voice sharp with hurt.

Silence stretched between them.

Then Talon turned to go.

Franco reached out, but didn't touch him.

"Talon…"

But Talon was already gone.

———

Clarice hung in silence, her magic humming beneath her skin.

Nerya had left the room. The emissary had not returned. She was alone—but not.

Because the Court was always there.

She could feel them in the stone. In the chains. In the voices behind the walls.

You are not theirs, they whispered. You are ours.

She closed her eyes, remembering Franco's touch, Talon's voice, the light of the moon over Valewind.

It felt like another life.

And her fire stirred again.

Not from pain.

From rage.

―――――

At midnight, Talon walked the cliff's edge where the fog curled like fingers.

Ysella found him there.

"She's alive," she said.

He didn't turn. "You're sure?"

"She's fighting."

He closed his eyes. "Then we go to her."

Ysella was quiet. "He won't forgive you if we're too late."

"I know."

"And if she does come back… she won't be the same."

Talon finally looked up. "Neither will we."

———

Far below, in the heart of the Crownless sanctum, Nerya returned to Clarice's chamber.

She unfastened the chains.

Clarice fell to her knees—but she didn't collapse.

She looked up, silver eyes blazing.

Nerya smiled. "Good. You're ready."

Clarice rose to her feet. "For what?"

"For the choice."

Nerya stepped aside, revealing a mirror of obsidian.

In it, Clarice saw herself—but older, darker, crowned in flame.

"You can stay with them," Nerya said. "Loved. Feared. Diminished."

"Or?"

"You can become what you were always meant to be."

Clarice reached for the mirror.

It pulsed in response.

And far above, Talon and Franco stood apart—staring into the night, not knowing that the next time they saw her, she might not return as the woman they knew.

Chapter 21: Through the Bones of the Earth

The descent into the earth began at dusk, when even the shadows seemed reluctant to stretch too far. Talon led the way, his boots echoing down the narrow stone steps carved into the ruined crypt beneath the old Bishop's Chapel. Franco followed close behind, silent, his blades strapped tightly across his back. Neither had spoken since the night before.

This was not a rescue driven by hope.

It was a reckoning.

The tunnels sloped downward into darkness so thick it clung to the skin. The walls wept moisture that tasted of salt and rust. Runes long abandoned by their creators pulsed faintly beneath layers of lichen, as if whispering warnings that would go unheard.

Ysella had found the entrance only hours earlier—drawn by blood wards left intentionally broken. The Crownless Court had wanted to be followed.

And that was what worried Talon most.

"They're luring us," he said as he placed a gloved hand against the damp stone.

Franco's voice was flat. "Let them try."

But even as he spoke, Talon could hear the strain. Not just in the words. In the pauses. In the weight Franco now carried in his silence.

They moved through a narrow gap flanked by carved skulls, the tunnel yawning wider into a vast chamber hollowed out long ago. A great ossuary spread before them—bones stacked in spirals, torchlight flickering off their hollow eyes. The air smelled of decay and burnt iron.

Then they heard it: chanting.

Low. Measured. In a tongue neither had heard in centuries.

Talon raised a hand and halted.

At the far end of the chamber, robed figures circled a dais built of fused vertebrae. At its center, Clarice knelt— unbound, but unmoving. Her eyes were closed. Her lips parted, whispering the same words as the others. Her skin shimmered faintly silver in the torchlight.

"She's chanting with them," Franco whispered.

"No," Talon said. "She's caught inside something."

A ritual.

Talon stepped forward.

The moment his boot struck the central stone, the chant stopped.

And Clarice opened her eyes.

They were no longer just silver.

They burned gold.

"Talon?" she said.

Franco moved beside him. "Clarice, we've come to—"

But she staggered back. "No. You shouldn't be here. It's not safe."

"Then let's leave together," Franco said, voice low, coaxing.

Behind them, the robed figures began to hiss.

"You can't stop it now," Clarice said, backing toward the dais. "I saw it. I felt it. She's already inside me."

"Fight her," Talon said. "Burn her out."

Clarice's voice trembled. "You don't understand—she doesn't want to take me. She wants me to want it."

Then the chamber shook.

A tremor from beneath.

Stone cracked. Bones fell from the walls.

And from the darkness behind the altar, Nerya stepped forward.

"Isn't this touching?" she said, voice smooth as oil. "The two men who love her, come to save her. But which one does she truly want?"

Franco unsheathed both blades. "I'll cut you down before you touch her."

"Oh?" Nerya said. "But she's already touched."

She raised a hand.

Clarice cried out, clutching her head.

Talon moved forward—fast.

But Nerya was faster.

She summoned a wave of black fire that flung him back across the chamber. Talon crashed into the bone wall, gasping as pain seared down his spine.

"Stop!" Clarice screamed.

The fire halted.

Franco caught Talon's shoulder. "Can you stand?"

Talon wiped blood from his mouth. "Try and stop me."

Clarice stood between them and her sister now.

"No more," she said.

Nerya tilted her head. "Then choose."

Clarice's voice was a whisper. "I already did."

Silver flame burst from her hands, striking the altar. The dais shattered, the runes breaking like glass. Screams erupted from the robed figures as the spell unraveled.

Nerya staggered back, snarling.

"You think you've won?" she hissed. "You've only opened the first door."

Clarice collapsed to her knees.

Franco rushed to her. Talon limped to the other side.

Together, they helped her stand.

"I'm sorry," she whispered. "I almost let it happen."

"You didn't," Franco said.

Talon met her eyes. "You came back."

But behind Clarice's eyes, something still flickered.

Something that hadn't fully left.

———

They emerged from the catacombs before sunrise.

Franco carried Clarice in his arms, her skin fever-hot, her lips silent.

Talon walked beside them, his coat torn, his steps slow.

Neither man spoke.

Because they both knew—

Clarice had come back.

But not whole.

And neither of them would be the same again.

Chapter 22: The Space Between Hearts

Clarice slept for two days.

Not the fevered, twitching rest of the wounded—but the deep, dreamless stillness of something being rewritten from the inside out. Her skin had cooled. The fire had quieted. But her eyes... even in sleep, they shifted beneath their lids, like something was still moving behind them.

She had returned from the Court's sanctum alive.

But not untouched.

And not unchanged.

Talon stood watch at the door of her tent. He hadn't left his post since they returned. He neither ate nor spoke. Only listened to the rustle of canvas, the flutter of her breath. Waiting for the moment she would wake—and waiting, deeper still, to know who she would be when she did.

Franco sat inside, just beside the bedroll. He held her hand, gently, as if afraid it might burn again. His eyes, red with sleeplessness, never left her face. He whispered stories from their travels: the crooked chimney in Dover, the orchard outside Marseille, the starlit run through the Carpathians. He spoke like a man casting a line into deep water, praying something would answer.

Talon watched him.

And knew it had already happened.

Not in a kiss. Not in a confession.

But in how Franco didn't turn to look for him anymore.

———

She stirred on the third morning.

Her lashes trembled, then lifted, and the silver glow of her eyes softened to smoke.

"Franco?" she rasped.

He was beside her in a second. "I'm here."

She blinked slowly. "You came."

"I never stopped."

Talon stepped into the doorway.

Clarice saw him. Her face didn't light up. But her breath caught.

"You too."

He nodded once. "You're safe."

"I'm not," she said. "But thank you for pretending I am."

Her eyes fluttered closed again.

Franco squeezed her hand.

Talon turned and left.

———

That evening, Talon sat alone atop the crumbling watchtower on the hill beyond the camp. He watched the torches flicker below, the ghosts of smoke curling up into the night. His thoughts were quiet. Not empty—never that —but suspended, like the space between breaths.

Franco climbed the tower slowly, his footfalls hesitant.

"You shouldn't be up here," he said.

Talon didn't move. "Neither should you."

They stood in silence.

Then Franco spoke. "She's waking up more. She asked for water. Asked about Ysella."

"Not about me?" Talon asked.

Franco winced. "She's still sorting things out."

Talon exhaled. "Aren't we all."

Franco came to stand beside him. "I'm not asking you to forgive me."

"There's nothing to forgive," Talon said. "Not yet."

Franco looked away. "Then what's left?"

Talon met his eyes. "I love you. But I don't know if we're the same men we were when this war started."

"We are," Franco said. "But we're also something else."

Talon nodded. "And she's part of that."

Franco's throat worked. "I didn't mean for it to happen."

"I know."

The wind blew through them, soft and cold.

Talon finally spoke again. "She'll need you in ways I never did."

"And you?" Franco asked. "What do you need?"

Talon gave a sad smile. "Time."

Franco touched his hand. Briefly. Then turned and descended the tower, step by slow step.

Talon stayed.

And let the wind carry the silence between them.

———

Clarice stood the next morning on her own.

She walked slowly through the tent flaps, blinking into the pale sun. Ysella met her, wrapping her in a shawl, saying nothing. There was nothing left to say that wouldn't reopen wounds.

Clarice looked across the field and saw the silhouette of Franco walking alone into the training circle. Then she turned and saw Talon, halfway across camp, watching her.

He didn't come closer.

She didn't move.

For now, this distance—this quiet—was all they could manage.

And behind them, beyond the hills, the ground stirred.

Because the Crownless were not finished.

And war would always return.

Chapter 23: The Quiet Flame

The wind had shifted. It no longer carried the weight of smoke or blood, but something subtler—like memory, or guilt.

Clarice stood at the edge of the ridge just past dawn, her cloak wrapped tightly around her frame. The mist curled up from the trees below, softening the sharp lines of the ruined battlefield beyond. Her breath caught with every inhale, not from cold, but from something that lived deeper now—something that hummed beneath her ribs like the echo of fire waiting to be summoned.

It had been four days since her return.

She had not yet stepped back into the war room. Had not lit a flame in front of the others. She hadn't even spoken to Talon.

And Franco... he was there, always near. Always watching.

But the air between them had changed.

She could feel it. In how he lingered longer than needed, but never too close. In how his eyes carried both devotion and distance. In how his hands trembled only when he thought she wasn't looking.

She didn't blame him.

She didn't know who she was now, either.

————

Franco paced the training field, his boots kicking up frost from the grass. He had practiced all morning—blade drills, defense patterns, counter forms he hadn't used since the siege of Lyon in 1678—but nothing stilled the noise in his chest.

He could still feel Clarice's fire when he closed his eyes. Not the warmth of it—no, warmth he had known. This was something else. Something older. Wilder.

The Clarice he carried in his arms from the catacombs was not the same woman who now walked the ridge in silence. She had returned with pieces missing. Or pieces added.

And yet, he loved her.

He loved her in a way he couldn't explain. Not like he loved Talon—not the same fierce, grounding passion that had lasted centuries—but in a way that made him feel like a part of something that hadn't yet been written. A story still unfolding.

And he hated himself for it.

He heard footsteps behind him and didn't need to turn to know who it was.

"You fight like you're trying to forget," Talon said.

Franco didn't pause. "Maybe I am."

Talon crossed his arms. "That never worked for you before."

Franco finally turned. "Nothing is working."

Their eyes met.

And something passed between them that had no name.

"I didn't come to accuse you," Talon said softly. "I came to ask what comes next."

Franco looked away. "That's the thing. I don't know anymore."

Talon nodded. "I do."

Franco's voice faltered. "What?"

"You'll stay with her. And I'll step back."

Franco's jaw tightened. "You don't get to decide that."

"I already have."

Silence.

Then Franco said the one thing Talon hadn't expected.

"She still dreams of you."

Talon blinked. "What?"

"In her sleep," Franco said. "She calls your name."

Talon swallowed. "That doesn't mean anything."

Franco stepped closer. "Doesn't it?"

———

Clarice sat with Ysella that afternoon in the silent grove just beyond the western barricade.

The older witch traced runes in the soil with her fingertip, not to cast—but to remember.

"You're not anchored anymore," Ysella said.

Clarice looked down at her hands. "I don't know what I'm holding on to."

"That's not what I mean," Ysella said. "Your soul is fraying. Your magic is bleeding into everything. If you don't ground yourself soon, you won't know what's you and what's… her."

Clarice's voice was small. "She's still inside me."

Ysella looked up. "But she's not stronger. You are."

Clarice didn't believe it.

Not yet.

———

That night, Talon stood atop the stone tower, watching the moon rise through the mist. He held a small locket in his hand—a token he hadn't touched in years. Inside it, a sketch Franco had drawn centuries ago: the two of them standing at the edge of the Danube, grinning like thieves who had outrun time.

He closed it gently.

"Do you regret it?" came Clarice's voice behind him.

He didn't turn. "What?"

"Loving him."

Talon let the question hang in the cold air.

"No," he said at last. "I regret not knowing how to let go."

Clarice stepped beside him, her cloak brushing his. "He still loves you."

"And he loves you."

Clarice's voice was steady. "That doesn't mean he's whole."

Talon finally turned to her. "And you?"

"I don't know what I feel," she admitted. "But I know I don't want to be the reason you lose him."

"You're not," Talon said. "Time is."

She touched his arm—just briefly.

Then left him to the moonlight.

———

The next morning, the Council reconvened.

This time, Clarice entered first.

She wore black.

Not the black of mourning.

But the black of choice.

"The Crownless are preparing to move again," she said. "I can feel them. They want war. And I want to give it to them."

Sir Cedric frowned. "You're not ready."

"I'm not asking your permission."

Clarice's voice was calm. Clear.

Talon stood slowly.

"She's right," he said. "We strike first. Before they do."

Franco looked between them.

He said nothing.

But when they left the tent, it was Clarice he followed.

Talon watched them go.

And let the silence return.

Chapter 24: The Fire at Her Back

The sky over London was the color of steel when Clarice crossed the southern barricade, flanked by twelve of the strongest bloodborn fighters from the allied clans. Her cloak, black with the silver insignia of Ysella's sigilwork sewn into the hem, whipped around her ankles like a storm's shadow. She didn't walk—she cut through the air with quiet command.

This wasn't the girl who once trembled in the presence of ancient power.

This was the woman who now carried it in her bloodstream.

Franco walked at her side, eyes alert, blades strapped high across his back. His movements were silent, confident, tethered to hers by something unseen and unspoken. They didn't speak as they marched—there was nothing left to say.

Talon stood at the gate, arms folded, watching them vanish into the fog.

He didn't call out.

He didn't ask to go.

But his hands remained clenched long after they disappeared.

———

The Crownless had been gathering near the remains of Grayfall Hollow—a crumbling stone monastery south of the Thames, abandoned for over a hundred years. Clarice had seen it in a vision three nights earlier—cold stone walls littered with runes older than any living tongue, and fire licking at the corners of a dream.

Now, it waited.

They moved like ghosts through the ruined orchard near the Hollow's edge. Clarice whispered the ward-breaking spell under her breath, and the magic melted before her like frost under fire. Franco raised his hand, signaling the others to wait.

Then, with Clarice at the center, they entered.

What they found was worse than expected.

There were no sentries. No traps. Just a silent circle of standing stones, recently dug up and reassembled. At its center stood a single figure—hooded, arms open.

The emissary.

"You come bold, fire-blood," he said, his voice like rusted metal.

Clarice stepped forward. "You summoned me."

He nodded. "And you answered."

Franco moved beside her. "Get behind me."

"No," she said. "This is mine."

The emissary removed his hood, revealing a face cracked with black veins, eyes empty hollows. "She is waiting, Clarice. You've heard her. You've felt her."

Clarice's hands flared silver. "I silenced her."

"But she speaks through you now," he whispered. "Would you like to know the truth of your lineage? Would you like to know what she kept from you?"

"Enough," Franco growled, stepping forward.

The emissary didn't flinch. "Strike me down, and the truth dies with me."

Clarice hesitated.

Franco didn't.

He lunged.

But before his blades reached their mark, the emissary vanished.

And the trap was sprung.

Dozens of Crownless rose from the ground—hidden beneath the shallow earth. Their skin cracked, eyes glowing, jaws unhinged. Clarice threw her hands wide, unleashing a wave of flame, but even as they burned, more came.

The fighters behind them charged. Blades met bone. Screams filled the Hollow.

Clarice stood her ground. Fire exploded from her hands, lighting up the sky—but her body trembled from the force of it. Franco defended her flank, moving like fury made flesh. But they were outnumbered.

And then they heard it.

Laughter.

Nerya stood at the far edge of the field, cloak dragging across the grass.

"Still you play with matches, sister," she called. "But will you burn for him?"

Clarice turned—just as a revenant broke past the line.

It struck Franco hard, slashing across his ribs. He staggered, blood soaking his shirt.

"No!" Clarice screamed, fire surging out of her in a blistering arc.

She incinerated everything within twenty feet—enemy and ally alike.

The battlefield went silent.

Smoke curled around her as she dropped to her knees beside Franco.

"I'm here," she whispered.

Franco's eyes fluttered. "You're too bright."

She held his face. "Don't you dare."

Talon arrived in a blur of movement, his sword cleaving down the last revenant behind her. He stood over them, breathing hard.

He looked at Clarice.

She looked at him.

There was blood on her hands.

Franco's blood.

And still, she burned.

———

Hours later, the survivors returned to camp. The Hollow was nothing but ash.

Franco lay in the infirmary tent, unconscious but stable. Ysella worked silently beside him, weaving ancient healing spells into the seams of his skin.

Clarice sat outside, her cloak damp with sweat and ash, hands trembling in her lap.

Talon stood nearby, watching her through the flame of the torchlight.

"You nearly lost him," he said quietly.

"I know."

"You could've burned everything."

"I did."

Talon crouched beside her.

"Clarice…" he began.

She looked at him. Her eyes were hollow.

"I don't know how to stop," she whispered.

Talon reached out, brushing a soot-smudge from her cheek. "Then maybe it's time I did."

She didn't understand.

But she would.

————

Inside the tent, Franco stirred.

His first word was her name.

And Talon heard it.

From the shadows.

He turned and walked into the dark.

Chapter 25: Where the Light Fractures

Franco woke to the scent of scorched linen and the echo of fire still whispering in his bones.

His eyes opened slowly. The ceiling above was canvas, sun-warmed and trembling from the wind. Pain lanced through his ribs as he tried to move, sharp and immediate. He groaned, and a shadow shifted beside him.

Clarice.

She was sitting in a wooden chair, cloak draped over her shoulders like a shield. Her hands were clasped tightly in her lap, fingers stained with blood—his and hers. She looked exhausted. Beautiful. Terrifying.

"Hey," she whispered.

He tried to smile. "You look like hell."

"I'm holding it back," she said, voice barely steady.

He looked down at his bandaged chest. "How bad?"

"Close." She swallowed. "Too close."

Franco reached out. She took his hand without hesitation.

"It was worth it," he said.

Clarice shook her head. "Don't say that."

"I'd do it again."

She looked away, jaw tightening. "That's what I'm afraid of."

————

Outside, Talon stood in the dying light.

He'd been standing there for hours.

Watching the tent. Listening to every sound. Every breath. Every whisper that drifted between them like threads of a world he no longer belonged to.

Ysella came to stand beside him.

"You should go in," she said.

He didn't look at her. "No."

"Why?"

"Because I'll want to stay."

Ysella didn't argue.

"You think she can hold it together?" he asked.

Ysella's voice was cautious. "If he stays with her, yes."

"And if he leaves?"

"Then she becomes the weapon they always feared she would be."

Talon said nothing.

But deep down, he already knew—

That weapon had already begun to form.

———

Later that night, Clarice walked through the camp alone.

The wind carried the scent of lavender and woodsmoke, the kind of night that could make you forget the world was ending. Her boots crunched over the frost-laced grass. Her mind burned with visions—Nerya's face, the emissary's laughter, Franco bleeding in her arms.

Talon stepped out from behind a post near the barracks.

"You shouldn't walk alone," he said.

She didn't startle. "You always find me."

"Not always," he said. "Not anymore."

She turned to him. "You're leaving."

He didn't deny it.

"You're not the one who runs," she said. "He is. Not you."

Talon looked at her, long and hard. "I've been running from this since the moment you arrived."

She blinked. "This?"

"You," he said. "Him. What's changing. What I'm losing."

Clarice stepped closer. "You haven't lost him."

Talon's voice cracked. "Haven't I?"

She reached out, touched his wrist.

There was still warmth between them. Still fire. Still grief.

And love.

But not enough to hold it together.

Not anymore.

"I never meant to take him," she whispered.

"You didn't," he said. "He chose."

Talon pulled back gently. "Take care of him."

Then he disappeared into the dark.

———

Franco awoke in the early hours before dawn.

Clarice was gone.

Talon was gone.

Only Ysella remained.

She placed a hand on his shoulder.

"They're moving against us again," she said.

He sat up slowly, pain sharp in his chest. "Where?"

"They've breached the southern outposts. But they didn't kill anyone."

Franco's brow furrowed. "Then what did they do?"

"They left a message."

She handed him a scrap of cloth. Black. Silken. Embroidered with a single phrase in crimson thread.

He walks alone.

Franco's heart dropped.

And he knew.

Talon had walked straight into them.

———

Deep in the marshlands past the burned woods, Talon moved like a ghost.

He had followed the trail all night—the scent of Crownless magic, of Nerya's illusion-binding smoke, of something ancient and waiting. His sword hung at his back, untouched. His face was calm.

He had not told anyone he was leaving.

Because this wasn't a mission.

It was surrender.

He reached the clearing as the sun broke the horizon.

And standing at the center, surrounded by stone obelisks older than the city itself, was Nerya.

"I wondered when you'd come," she said.

Talon didn't answer.

She smiled. "The fire has chosen her. And the blood has chosen him. So what's left for you, Talon of the Hollowed Clans?"

He drew his sword. "Me."

She nodded once. "Good."

Then everything went black.

———

Back at camp, Clarice returned to find Franco suiting up.

"You're not strong enough," she said.

"I'm going."

"Where?"

He looked at her. "To bring him back."

Clarice stared at him.

And for the first time, truly understood what she had broken.

Not through cruelty.

But through love.

"We'll go together," she said.

But inside, she feared—

They might already be too late.

Chapter 26: The Hollow Crown

Talon awoke in silence.

No chains. No torchlight. Just darkness.

The kind that lives beneath the skin of the world.

His limbs were heavy, his thoughts slower than usual—not from sleep, but from something darker. A spell. One he hadn't recognized until it had already crept beneath his defenses.

The Crownless didn't want him dead.

They wanted him listening.

He sat up slowly, blinking into the black. The chamber was vast, circular. The stone beneath him hummed faintly with blood magic. Runes carved into the walls pulsed red, slow as a heartbeat. The silence was not empty—it was waiting.

"Talon of the Hollowed Clans," came Nerya's voice from the dark.

He didn't flinch. "Speak plainly. I've had enough riddles."

She emerged from the shadows like a stain blooming through silk—elegant, deadly, eternal. She wore no crown now. She was the crown.

"I did not bring you here to torment you," she said, circling him. "You came of your own will."

"I came to end this."

"No," she said gently. "You came to see if you were already gone."

Talon rose to his feet, muscles slow to respond. "Try your illusions on someone else."

Nerya stepped closer. "You gave them everything. And still they left you behind."

His jaw clenched.

"They will forget you in time," she said. "The boy who carries your heart will follow hers now. And she—oh, she is becoming something beautiful. And terrifying."

Talon's voice was ice. "And you think I'll betray them because I'm broken?"

"No," Nerya said. "I think you'll join me because you're tired."

He stepped forward, the sword at his back gleaming faintly.

"I carry three centuries in these bones," he said. "And I would carry more years if it meant keeping them safe."

She smiled. "Then we'll see what's left of you when I'm done."

And with a snap of her fingers, the pain began.

Not physical.

Memory.

He was back in the fields of Valewind, watching Franco bleed. Back in the snow of Bucharest, watching an old lover turn to ash. Back beneath the altar in Florence in 1483, when Luciano had leaned down and whispered, "This is not death—it is clarity."

And then, just a few years later, a dim pub in Florence— where Franco had sat across from him with a crooked smile and tired eyes and said, "If you're offering me forever, I won't run."

All the pain. All the loss.

"Let it break you," Nerya whispered.

But Talon gritted his teeth and whispered, "No."

And the darkness trembled.

Clarice and Franco moved swiftly through the flooded tunnels beneath the South Wards. The last known signature of Talon's passage had flickered from here— blood magic residue, barely traceable. Clarice's fingers brushed the damp stone, eyes silver-bright.

"He's close," she said.

Franco's voice cracked. "You're sure?"

She turned to him. "Yes."

He nodded, but the silence between them remained heavy. He hadn't asked about Talon's last words. Clarice hadn't offered.

Some truths were too cruel, even for lovers.

The passage narrowed. They lit no torches—the fire lived inside Clarice now. Every step she took illuminated the way.

They reached the chamber entrance just as the screams began.

Franco froze. "That's him."

Clarice's jaw tightened. "It's not physical pain. She's using memory."

Franco stepped forward. "Then let's remind him who he is."

———

Inside the chamber, Talon fell to his knees.

Nerya circled him slowly, one hand trailing glowing ash behind her.

"You could have been eternal beside me," she said.

He looked up, sweat and blood streaking his face. "I already am."

Then Clarice's voice cut through the air.

"Let him go."

Nerya turned. Her smile widened. "And here comes the fire."

Clarice stepped into the chamber, flames curling around her hands.

Franco followed, blades drawn.

Nerya spread her arms. "Will you kill me now, little sister?"

"No," Clarice said. "You'll burn."

The flames leapt from her fingers—gold and silver now, braided and sharp. They struck Nerya's shield hard, but she didn't flinch.

Franco raced past, dragging Talon up from the floor.

"Easy," he whispered.

Talon opened his eyes. "You came."

"Of course," Franco said.

Clarice's fire intensified—matching Nerya's dark magic beat for beat.

But Nerya laughed.

"You're not ready," she said. "You still fight for love. For loyalty. That's why you'll lose."

Clarice's voice was low. "Not lose. End you."

Then, with a final burst of flame, Clarice severed the rune ring around the chamber.

The spell broke.

The memory assault fractured.

And the chamber shook.

Nerya staggered back, momentarily stunned.

Clarice's flames dimmed.

Talon stood on his own, bloodied but breathing.

He looked at Clarice. Then at Franco.

"I thought I was already gone," he said softly.

Clarice stepped closer. "You're still here."

Franco took Talon's hand.

"We're not finished," he said.

And Talon smiled—just slightly.

"No," he whispered. "We're not."

————

They fled as the chamber collapsed.

Outside, beneath the full moon, Talon inhaled the air like a man reborn.

Clarice watched him quietly.

Franco did not let go of his arm.

And somewhere in the dark behind them, Nerya opened her eyes again.

Not defeated. Just waiting.

Chapter 27: The Breaking Tide

The night air turned sick with ash.

It swept through the streets of London like a curse, curling through alleys and across rooftops, stirring unease in every corner of the city. The wind itself seemed to howl with voices—ancient, wordless, grief-hungry. By the time the first flames rose from the southern watch posts, Talon was already standing in the bell tower.

He saw them coming before anyone else.

Not an army. Not this time.

A tide.

They emerged from the sewers and bone tunnels, their bodies half-wrapped in rotting robes, eyes burning with void light. These were not revenants—they were awakened. Ancient creatures, long buried by pact and silence, unearthed by Nerya's rituals.

The final strike had begun.

And it was not war.

It was ruin.

———

Clarice burst into the war tent, flames flickering at her heels.

"They've breached the western rim," she said. "The Crownless are inside the city."

Franco stood over the maps, sword already in hand. "How many?"

She looked up, pale. "Too many to count."

Talon entered behind her, blood still drying on his collar from their escape days earlier. He didn't speak right away —he only placed his hand on the hilt of his blade and stared at the burning markers along the riverfront.

"They want her," he said. "Not the clans. Not the land. Her."

Clarice didn't deny it. "Then we end it."

Talon turned to her. "You've barely recovered."

"And if we wait, there'll be nothing left to recover."

Their eyes locked—his filled with years, hers filled with fire.

Franco stepped between them.

"Then we do this together," he said. "One last time."

Talon nodded, slowly. "One last time."

They moved through the city like firelight—Clarice burning from within, Franco silent but deadly at her side, and Talon... quiet, distant, already beginning to disappear from their world.

The first clash came at Covent Square.

The awakened screamed like wind through glass, their limbs too long, too fast. Magic hissed from their fingers like tar. Clarice raised her arms and met them with silver-gold flame, carving light through the shadows. Her magic didn't burn now—it shaped. The fire obeyed her. Because she no longer feared what it might take from her.

Franco danced through the chaos, blades glinting red under moonlight. He fought to protect her—but she no longer needed protection.

Talon moved apart from them. He didn't rush in. He hunted.

When he found the emissary, it was in the shell of an old cathedral, where stained glass windows shattered in protest of the darkness seeping through their stone.

"You followed," the emissary said.

"I never left," Talon replied—and drove his sword through the creature's spine.

But even as the body crumbled, the emissary whispered with its last breath:

You will.

―――――

The fighting raged for hours. The air turned red with smoke, and London trembled beneath the weight of war. But by dawn, the awakened began to fall.

Not because they were overpowered.

Because they were spent.

A final scream echoed from the crypt of Blackmoor Square, and then silence rippled through the streets like the first breath after drowning.

It was over.

The Crownless Court had fallen.

But their queen still lived.

And she was watching.

―――――

Back at camp, the wounded rested. The survivors buried the fallen. Clarice stood over a pyre, flame dancing quietly in her palm. She did not cry.

Franco stood beside her.

"Where is he?" she asked.

Franco didn't answer.

But he knew.

Talon stood atop the far wall overlooking the city.

He hadn't spoken to either of them since the last blow was struck. His coat was tattered, his face grim.

Clarice approached quietly.

"You're not staying," she said.

"No," he replied.

"Is it her?"

"No," he said again. "It's me."

She nodded.

"You saved us," she whispered.

He turned to her. "I just delayed the end."

Then she hugged him—and this time, he let her.

"Thank you," she said.

He stepped back. "Take care of him."

And before the sun could rise, he was gone.

———

Franco found a note on his cot. No signature.

Just a single line:

When you look up, I'll be watching the same sky.

And in the distance, the road west beckoned.

Chapter 28: Ashes and Embers

The smoke had thinned, but it hadn't vanished. It lingered in alleyways and drifted over rooftops like a fading curse, staining the dawn with memory. The Crownless Court was gone, burned back into shadow. But what remained was not peace. It was silence. A hollow quiet, unfamiliar and unwelcome.

Clarice stood at the edge of the camp, her back to the rising sun, her arms wrapped around herself—not from cold, but from the ache that bloomed inside her chest like something unspoken. Around her, the wounded were tended to, pyres still glowed dimly, and the clans worked in solemn unity to repair what little remained of their alliance.

But she was alone.

And she felt it.

Franco approached quietly, his boots crunching over cinders and frost. He stopped just behind her, not touching her, but close enough to share the air.

"He left in the dark," she whispered.

"I know."

"You let him."

"I had to."

Clarice turned. Her eyes, bright with magic now fully awakened, shimmered—but not with tears. "He didn't even say goodbye."

Franco's voice broke. "He did."

He handed her the note—creased, folded tight, the edges singed as if even paper had struggled to hold onto Talon's words.

She read it silently, then closed her hand over it.

"I don't know if I'm angry," she said.

"You're grieving."

She looked up at him, the fire behind her gaze momentarily soft. "And you?"

"I've been grieving him since we left Florence."

That, she understood.

They stood in the quiet a moment longer. The world still turning without the man who had anchored them both.

———

That evening, the clans held what remained of their final council.

The great tent, half-collapsed, smelled of blood and burnt parchment. The banners of Valewind and Ironroot hung in tatters. Dame Elira stood in place of her fallen brother. Sir Cedric leaned heavily on a cane, his armor stained and cracked. Lady Evangeline had not returned from the battlefield—her sword had been found near the mouth of the Whisperer's catacomb, embedded in stone.

Clarice stepped forward. Not as heir. Not as a pawn.

As the one who survived.

"I don't speak for Talon Bellini," she said. "But I carry what he left behind. And I say this: the war is not over. The name Crownless is buried, but the rot remains. We rebuild. We prepare. And we never again ignore the shadows at our feet."

None challenged her.

Not even the old guard.

Franco watched her from the back of the room, arms crossed, chest aching. He saw the strength in her. The clarity. But it made his own path all the more unclear.

Because Talon had always been the reason.

And now he was gone.

That night, Clarice found Franco alone in the ruined courtyard.

He sat beneath a stone archway, a bottle of red wine in one hand, a dagger in the other, twirling it idly as if trying to remember what it had ever meant to be a warrior instead of just… wounded.

She sat beside him without asking.

"You don't sleep much," she said.

"Didn't sleep much before."

She reached for the wine and drank from the bottle, not bothering with a glass.

"You'll go after him, won't you?" she asked quietly.

"I don't know."

"You do."

Franco looked at her, and for the first time in weeks, there was no tension between them—only ache. A shared ache. She placed her hand over his.

"I loved him too," she whispered.

"I know."

And in that quiet moment, the pain was no longer a divide —it was a thread. Worn, but still connecting them.

He looked to the east. "He's probably halfway to the New World by now."

"He'll wait," she said. "He always did."

———

Elsewhere, far beyond the reach of England's coast, a ship cut through fog-thick waters under a moonless sky. Talon stood at the bow, coat billowing in the salt-laced wind, his eyes fixed on the horizon.

New Orleans.

The word sounded strange in his mind—foreign, heavy with promise.

He had nothing with him but a small satchel, a journal, and a locket with no image inside.

Behind him, the captain muttered to his crew in French, the sails creaking with every gust.

Talon didn't turn. He didn't sleep.

He watched.

The world was changing. And he would not be left behind.

Chapter 29: The Echoes We Keep

Rain fell softly over London that night. Not the kind that howled or stormed, but a quiet, persistent drizzle—as if the sky, too, had grown weary of holding back. The city was healing, but beneath its stone and soot, the cracks ran deep.

Franco stood alone beneath the eaves of the ruined chapel that once served as a safe house for their allies. Its stained-glass windows had shattered weeks ago, and shards of color littered the flagstone like frozen tears. He didn't know why he'd returned—only that something pulled him here, as if memory itself had summoned him.

He clutched the locket in his hand—the one Talon had left behind. Empty. No portrait. No keepsake. Just the hollow weight of absence.

Behind him, footsteps.

Clarice.

She didn't speak, not right away. She stepped beside him, wrapped in a long coat, her hair braided back with a black ribbon soaked from the rain.

"He's really gone," she said softly.

Franco didn't answer.

"I can still feel him," she added, her voice steadier than her eyes. "Like the echo of thunder after the lightning has already passed."

Franco exhaled sharply through his nose. "He was never meant to stay forever. Not here."

Clarice tilted her head. "But you were."

That silence between them cracked then, and for a long time, neither moved. The chapel wept quietly around them.

"I don't know who I am without him," Franco said at last, his voice low. "We spent three centuries side by side. I knew his breath, his rage, his quiet joy. I knew the way he watched a sunrise he couldn't feel. I knew the way he kept one hand on the hilt even when no one was looking."

"You were his soul," Clarice said. "But even souls must take separate paths to survive."

She turned and walked into the nave, trailing her fingers along the weathered pews. Franco followed slowly.

"There's something you need to see," she said. "Something he left for you."

At the altar, tucked beneath a loose stone, she produced a small bundle—wrapped in oilcloth, tied in crimson thread. She handed it to Franco with care.

Inside, there was a journal.

Talon's handwriting filled the pages, every letter a blade, every sentence a wound dressed in memory. Franco flipped through it, devouring the words without speaking.

One page stopped him cold:

I cannot ask him to follow me to America. He belongs here. With her. With the future. I've only ever known how to survive. But perhaps now... I need to learn how to be alone again. Perhaps it's time he learns to be more than just my shadow.

Franco closed the book slowly.

"I should hate him for this," he whispered.

"But you don't," Clarice said gently.

"No," he said. "I love him even more for it."

———

Elsewhere in London, the clans held one final gathering before dissolving into legend once more. Their alliances had grown thin, but their shared scars would remain.

Lady Seraphina had not returned from the last skirmish. Rumors whispered she had fled to the continent.

Dame Elira returned to Silverbrook to bury her brother in sacred ground.

Sir Cedric's health waned—he passed the Moonveil crest to a younger generation.

Clarice was named Warden of the East—protector of what remained. And Franco?

Franco declined all titles.

He remained at the periphery, ever watchful. And when asked where Talon Bellini had gone, he would only say: "Where legends go to rest."

———

Weeks later, Clarice stood in the undercroft of their former sanctuary—now hers.

A map of the world was pinned to the stone wall, dotted with markings, coordinates, trails. She traced a slow line across the Atlantic.

New Orleans.

A strange, wild place. French. Spanish. English with a strange dialect. A city of trade and secrets and heat.

And vampires, already whispered about in the shadows.

She placed her finger there, her thoughts drifting like the sails of Talon's ship.

"I'll find you," she whispered to no one.

"I'm not ready to let you go."

———

Far from London, Talon walked the deck of a ship now docked in the harbor of New Orleans. The scent of the city rose thick and cloying—sweet magnolia, sweat, rum, blood.

He stepped onto the gangplank as the sun dipped behind the Mississippi.

He was not the same man who had once stood beneath the archways of Florence. Nor the same vampire who had led armies beneath London's gaslit haze.

He was older now. Weary.

But unbroken.

He would rebuild. Disappear for a time. Let the world forget.

Because someday, they would remember again.

And when they did—Talon Bellini would be ready.

Chapter 30: Beneath the Silence of Ash

The fog clung to London like a final breath—thick, cold, and slow to lift. Along the banks of the Thames, the river whispered its eternal song, lapping gently at the stone piers as though it, too, mourned the turning of a page.

Talon stood at the edge of the dock. His coat, black and finely tailored, hung motionless despite the breeze that wound its way down from the city above. The lantern beside him flickered dimly, casting his shadow long across the wood, warping with every heartbeat.

Behind him, London slumbered in uneasy peace.

Franco was not there.

He hadn't come to say goodbye.

Not in person.

Instead, a single red lily had been left at Talon's door that morning—silent, fragrant, and blooming despite the frost.

It was enough.

Talon's eyes lifted toward the dark horizon, where a ship sat tethered and ready. Its sails had not yet been raised, but the crew moved like ghosts along its deck, preparing for the long voyage across the Atlantic. He would depart under the veil of night, just as he had always arrived—in shadow, with purpose.

He turned slowly, taking one final look at the city he had both protected and bled for.

Every alley held a memory.
Every rooftop echoed with footsteps of war.
Every stone knew his name.

But it was no longer his.

London would go on. So would Franco. So would Clarice.

But Talon Bellini… he would vanish for a time.

Just as he had done once before, when Florence drowned in blood and betrayal.

Just as he would do again, and again, until the world forgot.

————

Clarice stood at the window of their townhouse, watching from a distance as the ship rocked gently against its moorings. The city stretched behind her like a wound she could not close.

She had not stopped him.

She couldn't.

She and Franco had not spoken much since the last gathering. Their conversations were brief—quiet exchanges loaded with everything left unsaid. She saw the sorrow in him, and the shame. She saw, too, the guilt that Talon carried in silence.

But she did not chase either of them.

She carried her own burden now.

The blood magic within her had begun to stir more violently with each passing moon. Whisperers had returned to her dreams. Some nights, she awoke to symbols carved into the frost on her window—none of which she remembered writing.

Still, she remained in London.

To protect.
To guide.
To remember.

As Talon had once done for her.

Franco stood at the far side of the room, silent, still. He watched the rain streak down the glass without blinking.

"He'll arrive in New Orleans within weeks," Clarice said softly.

Franco gave the smallest nod.

"You could have gone."

"No," he said. "He needed to leave without me."

Clarice turned toward him, her eyes searching his profile.

"Then why are you still here?"

Franco met her gaze, and for the first time since Talon's departure, he looked… lost.

"I don't know who I am now."

She walked to him, placed her hand on his cheek. "Then let's find out together."

––––––

The ship creaked as Talon stepped aboard. The deckhands gave him a wide berth—not out of fear, but respect. They knew he was not merely a man. There was something in his bearing, in the silence that clung to him like a second skin.

He descended below deck into his private quarters. It was sparsely furnished. A single trunk. A glass case that held a dagger once used in the Valley of Ash. A painting— Franco's hand—of the forest that had nearly swallowed them both.

He sat at the desk, opened a fresh journal, and dipped the pen in ink.

March 1st, 1806.
London sleeps behind me. New Orleans calls.
I carry their names with me—the living and the dead.
I do not know what I will become in the years ahead.
But I know who I have been.

He paused, let the ink dry.

Outside, the fog began to thin. A bell rang.

The sails caught wind.

The ship groaned as it pulled away from the dock.

And just before London disappeared from view, Talon stepped once more into the night air, his eyes forward.

A new world awaited him.

One of jazz, and blood, and secrets buried in southern soil.

He was not done.

Not yet.

THE END

ABOUT THE AUTHOR

With the completion of Robert Austin Mowbray's seventh novel, Inheritance of Ash, the fourth installment in the Vampire Talon series, he invites readers on an imaginative journey through the centuries, spanning from the 15th to the 21st. The completed novels, along with four more planned for the future, allow Robert to explore the rich experiences of Talon as he navigates the complexities of time, identity, and the supernatural.

Robert's passion for ancient European cultures and cities fuels his research, immersing readers in vibrant historical settings that make his stories come alive. His writing not only delves into the world of vampires but also transports readers to eras where they can vividly envision the sights, sounds, and emotions of the past.

In addition to his literary pursuits, Robert is an accomplished painter. His artworks, celebrated for their depth and creativity, can be found adorning gallery walls in both Rome and Paris. A recipient of numerous international awards, Robert's masterpieces have also been featured in prestigious art books and magazines throughout Europe.

Join Robert on this captivating journey as he continues to weave tales that blend history, art, and the eternal allure of the vampire mythos, inviting you to experience the extraordinary alongside his unforgettable characters, one story at a time.

ROBERT AUSTIN MOWBRAY
AUTHOR'S BOOKS

In Full View: The Unveiling

Victor Salvatore: The Making of a Mastermind

Canvas of Shadows

The Vampire Talon

The Tiny Donkey Trio

The Vampire Talon: Dante's Wrath

The Vampire Talon: Franco's Ascension